Dostoyevsky Bilingual

Edited by Olga Kuzmina and Sarah Young

Originally published as issue #24 of the journal *Chtenia*.

Cover: Portrait of Fedor Dostoyevsky by Vasily Perov, 1872.

ISBN 978-1-880100-24-0

StoryWorkz, Inc.
73 Main Street, Suite 402
Montpelier, VT 05602
storyworkz.com

Dostoyevsky's Death Mask
1881

Contents

The Many Faces of Fyodor Mikhailovich
Sarah Young

Fyodor Mikhailovich Dostoyevsky (1821-1881) is often regarded as the stereotypical Russian novelist: the author of huge, intense, philosophical works that make it onto every list of the world's greatest novels, but are perhaps few people's idea of fun. But this reputation ignores the great variety of his writing. His major novels are indeed long, profound meditations on humanity, and on good and evil, but they are also real page-turners. Their plots revolve around murder, sexual jealousy, political intrigue, and family strife, and their characters – from the most vicious to the most saintly – represent all the extremes of human nature, behavior and experience. Like his anti-hero Raskolnikov in *Crime and Punishment*, who theorizes about the division of humanity into the "extraordinary" and the "ordinary" and seeks to count himself among the former, Dostoyevsky wasn't interested in the average or the mundane.

But this serious side often incorporates a good deal of humor and satire. In his novels, buffoons, such as the inveterate liar General Ivolgin and the apocalyptic interpreter Lebedev in *The Idiot*, frequently steal the show with their hilarious outpourings. Scandalous crowd scenes create

a sense of heightened tension, but the inappropriate behavior they feature, as at the funeral meal for Marmeladov in *Crime and Punishment*, which descends into a melée of drunken abuse, makes these episodes very funny as well. A number of his short stories take scandal as the basis for more purely humorous writing, from the farcical tale of marital infidelity "Another Man's Wife and a Husband under the Bed," whose title – possibly my favorite in the whole of Russian literature – says it all, to the comedy of embarrassment in "A Nasty Anecdote," in which a high-level civil servant gate-crashes the wedding of one of his minions and creates havoc by getting horrifically drunk.

"The Crocodile," included in this collection, represents another side of Dostoyevsky 's humor, as it satirizes the fashionable ideas of the day. But the story's scenario – a man being swallowed whole by a crocodile, only to envisage remaining there and becoming an intellectual phenomenon – also tells us that we are far from the realism we associate with most of Dostoyevsky's peers. He saw himself not as a psychologist, but as a "realist in a higher sense," regarding "reality" as encompassing all aspects of human experience, including the psychic dimension. To incorporate this, he developed an artistic method that enabled the absurd and eccentric to sit side-by-side with the actual, that allowed embodied characters simultaneously to be emanations of other characters' minds or souls, and that explored the unconscious mind and the perception of other worlds, whether in the form of hallucinations and nightmares, the appearance of ghosts, or religious experience. "My idealism is more real than their realism," he stated of the utilitarian approach to literature touted by his radical opponents, citing real-life events, such as the murder of a pawnbroker by a student, which his "fantastic" fiction had apparently predicted.

As this suggests, alongside his exploration of realms beyond the everyday, Dostoyevsky maintained an avid interest in current affairs. His fiction persistently debated with and criticized the ideas of the

radical journalists and ideologues who held sway amongst Russia's intelligentsia. He sought out stories in the press about crimes, and incorporated references to them in his novels, using them to locate his timeless investigations of human nature firmly in the present day. And he commented in his many journalistic articles on current events, from the cultural (regularly publishing his reflections on art exhibitions and critiques of new publications) to the social (contemporary court cases, especially those involving women defendants or child victims, were a specific interest), to the geopolitical (the Russo-Turkish war in particular became a vehicle for the advancement of the author's increasingly xenophobic Orthodox nationalism in his later years).

Dostoyevsky's life was almost as turbulent as his fiction. The death sentence he received, the hard labor he endured, a disastrous pact with a publisher, which almost destroyed his career, years of exile from his native country, a passion for gambling that lasted several years, and long-term serious illness in the form of epilepsy, all contributed to his fictional imagination, but also disrupted his life significantly. Unlike most writers at the time, including his fellow novelists Tolstoy and Turgenev, Dostoyevsky was not independently wealthy, and his writing and publishing activities represented his only regular source of income. This gave an added urgency to his work – the need to attract readers was paramount – and makes it all the more remarkable that he produced works that are not only literary classics, but have also made major contributions to political, moral, and religious philosophy, as well as to areas of knowledge as diverse as medicine and the law.

With such a varied life, and so many different aspects of his writing to cover, and a *Complete Works* that fills thirty stout volumes, this bilingual volume can provide only a snapshot of Dostoyevsky's writing. Instead of his best known works, which are readily accessible in numerous good translations, the selections – extracts from two letters, two journalistic articles, a diary entry, and an abridged story – have

been chosen to reflect different aspects of Dostoyevsky's writing at key moments in his life. Their aim is to introduce readers who already know Dostoyevsky's major novels to texts they may not have come across, and to show new readers that he is a more accessible author than his reputation may suggest. I hope for both groups that these readings will spark, or renew, an interest, and lead to further exploration of this extraordinary writer's work.

London, August 2013

Contributors

FYODOR DOSTOYEVSKY (1821-1881) used his novels to peer into the tortured depths of the human soul. Over the course of his difficult life, Dostoyevsky went from a confirmed revolutionary-socialist to a religious arch-conservative, managing to express through his literature all of the ideas and theories which enraptured, ennerved and invigorated Russian society in the middle of the nineteenth century.

CONSTANCE GARNETT (1861-1946) was a legendary translator of some 70 works of nineteenth century Russian literature, and was one of the first translators into English of Dostoyevsky and Chekhov. She was drawn to the profession after a trip to Russia in 1893, when she met Lev Tolstoy at Yasnaya Polyana.

NORA FAVOROV has been struggling for decades to figure out the best way to express Russian thought in literate and natural English, a game she considers more entertaining than any crossword puzzle. Most of her translation work these days – including her regular task of translating *Russian Life* magazine's Calendar feature – centers around her favorite subject, Russian history. She is associate editor of *SlavFile*, a newsletter for Slavic translators and interpreters.

KENNETH LANTZ is Professor Emeritus of Slavic Languages and Literatures at the University of Toronto and a specialist in nineteenth-century Russian literature. He is the author of *The Dostoevsky Encyclopedia* (Westport, CT: Greenwood Press, 2004). His translation of Dostoevsky's *Writer's Diary* was awarded the AATSEEL Translation Prize for 1993.

LYDIA RAZRAN STONE is a first generation American who works as a technical and literary translator from Russian into English. She earned a Ph.D. in Cognitive Psychology and spent 10 years working for NASA, tracking and writing about Soviet biomedical research relevant to space flight. Her first bilingual book of translations, a poetry collection by Irina Ratushinskaya entitled *Wind of the Journey*, was published in 2000 by Cornerstone Press. Many of her translations have been published in various venues and her translated plays have been performed. She is the editor of *SlavFile*, the publication of the Slavic Language Division of the American Translators Association, for which she writes a humor and cultural column. Her translation of Krylov's fairy tales, *The Frogs Who Begged for a Tsar (and 61 other Russia fables by Ivan Krylov)* was published by Russian Life Books.

EUGENIA SOKOLSKAYA came to the United States from Russia when she was four. In addition to a normal public-school education, she also received extensive instruction in Russian literature, film, and history from her parents. She is now a graduate of Swarthmore College and a freelance translator. In 2011, she was short-listed for the Rossica Young Translators Award.

SARAH YOUNG is a lecturer in Russian at the School of Slavonic and East European Studies, University College London. She previously held posts at the University of Toronto and the University of Nottingham. She is the author of *Dostoevsky's 'The Idiot' and the Ethical Foundations of Narrative*, and co-editor of *Dostoevsky on the Threshold of Other Worlds*. Her current projects expand her research on Dostoyevsky into new areas: she is writing a study of Russian labor camp narratives, and developing a literary cartography project, Mapping St Petersburg (mappingpetersburg.org). She blogs about her research and teaching at sarahjyoung.com.

Portrait in Pencil
Konstantin Trutovsky, 1847

The Petersburg Feuilletons
Fyodor Dostoyevsky

In 1847 Dostoyevsky was at the start of his literary career, having just published *Poor Folk* to great acclaim and *The Double* to a critical mauling. In addition to his fictional works, he began writing journalistic pieces, as he would throughout his career, which equally contributed to the development of his literary voice. The "Petersburg Feuilletons," a series of four articles published in the newspaper *St. Petersburg Gazette (Sankt-Peterburgskie vedomosti),* are very much a product of the times: playful sketches in a conversational style that tap into the "Natural School" vogue for "slice of life" descriptions of ordinary people and situations. Their subject matter, Petersburg, its inhabitants and mores, indicate the importance of the city that becomes a character in its own right in much of Dostoyevsky's fiction. Here he discusses the "dreamer," the quintessential bookish Petersburg type who loses contact with reality because of the hallucinatory nature of the city.

June 15, 1847

… If a person is dissatisfied, if he lacks the means to express himself and show what is best in him (not out of pride, but simply due to the most natural human need to recognize, realize, and define one's Self in real life), he immediately winds up involving himself in an incident of the most unbelievable sort, or, if I may, will turn to drink, or lapse into card playing and cheating, or become pugnacious, or, in the end, will go mad from ambition while in his heart despising ambition and even suffering from the fact that he has been compelled to suffer due to something as trifling as ambition. You look on, and cannot help but draw a conclusion that is almost unjust, even offensive, but that appears extremely plausible, that we are little aware of our own merit, that we do not have as much egoism as we need, and that, in the end, we're simply not used to doing a good deed without any reward. Assign some task, for example, to a conscientious, systematic German, a task that is contrary to all his aspirations and inclinations, and simply make him see that this activity will set him on his way, will keep him and his family fed, for example, will earn him a place in society, will take him to his desired goal and so forth, and the German will immediately set to work on this task, will even complete it without demur, and will even introduce some special, new system into his work.

15 июня 1847

… Коль неудовлетворён человéк, коль нет срéдств емý вы́сказаться и проявúть то, что полýчше в нем (не из самолю́бия, а вслéдствие сáмой естéственной необходúмости человéческой сознáть, осуществúть и обуслóвить своё Я в действúтельной жúзни), то сейчáс же и впадáет он в какóе-нибýдь сáмое невероя́тное собы́тие; то, с позволéния сказáть, сопьётся, то пýстится в картёж и шýлерство, то в бретёрство, то, наконéц, с умá сойдёт от амбúции, в то же сáмое врéмя вполнé про себя́ презирáя амбúцию и дáже страдáя тем, что пришлóсь страдáть úз-за такúх пустякóв, как амбúция. И смóтришь — невóльно дойдёшь до заключéния почтú несправедлúвого, дáже обúдного, но óчень кáжущегося вероя́тным, что в нас мáло сознáния сóбственного достóинства; что в нас мало необходúмого эгоúзма и что мы, наконéц, не привы́кли дéлать дóброе дéло без вся́кой награ́ды. Дáйте, напримéр, какóе-нибýдь дéло аккурáтному, системати́ческому нéмцу, дéло, протúвное всем егó стремлéниям и наклóнностям, и растолкýйте тóлько емý, что э́та дéятельность вы́ведет егó на дорóгу, прокóрмит, напримéр, и егó и семéйство егó, вы́ведет в лю́ди, доведёт до желáемой цéли и т. д., и нéмец тотчáс прúмется за дéло, дáже беспрекослóвно окóнчит егó, дáже введёт какýю-нибудь осóбенную, нóвую систéму в своё заня́тие. Но хорошó ли э́то? Отчáсти и нет; потомý

But is that a good thing? Not entirely; because in that case man reaches another, horrifying extreme, a phlegmatic fixity that at times completely excludes the man and includes in his place a system, obligation, a formula, and an unconditional worship of the ways of our forefathers, even though the ways our forefathers did things do not befit the present century. The reforms of Peter the Great, which created free activity in Rus, would have been impossible if our national character had such an element, an element that oftentimes takes the form of the naively beautiful, but at others the form of the excessively comic. We have seen that the German will wait patiently until the age of fifty to marry his betrothed, meanwhile teaching the children of the Russian gentry, saving his kopeks, and finally coming together in lawful matrimony with his heroically faithful Minchen, withered from long years of maidenhood. A Russian would not hold out that long; he'd sooner fall out of love or let himself go or do something else – and here one can quite truthfully state the reverse of the famous saying: What's good for the German is death to the Russian. And are there many of us Russians who have the resources to do their work with love, as it should be done; because any task requires eagerness, requires love in the doer, requires the whole person. Are there many, in the end, who have found their activity? And some activities furthermore require resources in advance, require that one be provided for, and a person might not be inclined toward any other task – he'll dismiss it with a wave of his hand and before you know it, the task lies in shambles. Then in characters that hunger for activity, hunger to live life first-hand, hunger for reality, but that are weak, effeminate, and delicate, there little by little arises something that goes by the name "dreaminess," and in the end a man is no longer a man, but some strange being of the neuter gender – a dreamer. And do you know what a dreamer is, gentlemen? It is a Petersburg nightmare, it is sin personified, it is a mute, mysterious, morose, and savage tragedy, complete with raving horrors, catastrophes, peripeteias, protases, and denouements – and we say this in all earnestness. You on occasion encounter a distracted man with a vaguely dim look in his eye, often with a pale, haggard face, always appearing as if he's engaged

что в э́том слу́чае челове́к дохо́дит до друго́й, ужаса́ющей кра́йности, до флегмати́ческой неподви́жности, иногда́ соверше́нно исключа́ющей челове́ка и включа́ющей на ме́сто его́ систе́му, обя́занность, фо́рмулу и безусло́вное поклоне́ние де́довскому обы́чаю, хотя́ бы де́довский обы́чай был и не в ме́рку настоя́щему ве́ку. Рефо́рма Петра́ Вели́кого, созда́вшая на Руси́ свобо́дную де́ятельность, была́ бы невозмо́жна с таки́м элеме́нтом в наро́дном хара́ктере, элеме́нтом, принима́ющим ча́сто фо́рму наи́вно-прекра́сную, но иногда́ чрезвыча́йно коми́ческую. Вида́ли, что не́мец до пяти́десяти лет сиди́т в жениха́х, у́чит дете́й у ру́сских поме́щиков, скола́чивает ко́е-каку́ю копе́йку и та́к совокупля́ется наконе́ц зако́нным бра́ком с свое́й пересо́хшей от до́лгого деви́чества, но геро́йски ве́рной Ми́нхен. Ру́сский не вы́держит, уж он скоре́е разлю́бит и́ли опу́стится, и́ли сде́лает что-нибудь друго́е — и здесь мо́жно дово́льно ве́рно сказа́ть наоборо́т изве́стной посло́вице: что не́мцу здоро́во, то ру́сскому смерть. А мно́го ли нас, ру́сских, име́ют сре́дства де́лать своё де́ло с любо́вью, как сле́дует; потому́ что вся́кое де́ло тре́бует охо́ты, тре́бует любви́ в де́ятеле, тре́бует всего́ челове́ка. Мно́гие ли, наконе́ц, нашли́ свою́ де́ятельность? А ина́я де́ятельность ещё тре́бует предвари́тельных средств, обеспече́нья, а к ино́му де́лу челове́к и не скло́нен — махну́л руко́й, и, смо́тришь, де́ло повали́лось из рук. Тогда́ в хара́ктерах, жа́дных де́ятельности, жа́дных непосре́дственной жи́зни, жа́дных действи́тельности, но сла́бых, же́нственных, не́жных, ма́ло-пома́лу зарожда́ется то, что называ́ют мечта́тельностию, и челове́к де́лается наконе́ц не челове́ком, а каки́м-то стра́нным существо́м сре́днего рода — мечта́телем. А зна́ете ли, что тако́е мечта́тель, господа́? э́то кошма́р петербу́ргский, э́то олицетворённый грех, э́то траге́дия, безмо́лвная, таи́нственная, угрю́мая, ди́кая, со все́ми нейсто́выми у́жасами, со все́ми катастро́фами, перипети́ями, завя́зками и развя́зками, — и мы говори́м э́то во́все не в шу́тку. Вы иногда́ встреча́ете челове́ка рассе́янного, с неопределённо-ту́склым взгля́дом, ча́сто с бле́дным, измя́тым лицо́м, всегда́ как бу́дто за́нятого чем-то ужа́сно тя́гостным, каки́м-то головоло́мнейшим де́лом, иногда́ изму́ченного, утомлённого как бу́дто от тя́жких трудо́в, но в су́щности не производя́щего

in some sort of terribly onerous and perplexing task, at times tormented, exhausted, as if from back-breaking labor, but who in essence produces nothing whatsoever – such is the outward appearance of the dreamer. The dreamer is always difficult because he is exceptionally changeable: he can be exceedingly cheerful, exceedingly gloomy, a boor, attentive and affectionate, an egoist, or capable of the most noble sentiments. In government service these gentlemen are good for absolutely nothing, and although they do hold such appointments, they are incapable of actually getting anything done and drag out their work, which is essentially almost worse than doing nothing. They regard any formalities with a profound sense of revulsion and, despite the fact that, or actually specifically because they are docile, peaceable, and fearful of any truble, they are more inclined to be formalists than anyone. But at home it is an entirely different matter. For the most part they settle into extreme seclusion in inaccessible corners, as if hiding themselves there from people and society and indeed, they make a rather melodramatic impression when one first lays eyes on them. They are sullen and taciturn with the servants and self-absorbed, but they adore all that is lazy, easy, contemplative, everything that has a soothing effect on the feelings or excites the senses. They love to read and to read any sort of books, even serious, specialized ones, but usually quit reading after the second or third page, since they are fully satisfied. Their imaginations are lively, volatile, easy, already excited, already tuned to impression, and an entire dreamlike world – complete with joys, sorrows, hell and heaven, captivating women, heroic feats, noble deeds, always with some sort of gigantic battle, crimes and various horrors – suddenly takes hold of the entire being of the dreamer. The room disappears, space also, time stops or flies by so quickly that an hour seems like a minute. Sometimes entire nights pass unnoticed in indescribable pleasures; often in a few hours a paradise of love or an entire enormous, gigantic, incredible, miraculous life is experienced like a dream, grandiose and beautiful. In accordance with some mysterious and tyrannical law, the pulse races, tears splatter, pale, moist cheeks burn with a febrile fire, and when the dawn flashes

ро́вно ничего́, — тако́в быва́ет мечта́тель снару́жи. Мечта́тель всегда́ тяжёл, потому́ что неро́вен до кра́йности: то сли́шком ве́сел, то сли́шком угрю́м, то грубия́н, то внима́телен и не́жен, то эгои́ст, то спосо́бен к благоро́днейшим чу́вствам. В слу́жбе э́ти господа́ реши́тельно не годя́тся и хоть и слу́жат, но всё-таки ни к чему́ не спосо́бны и то́лько тя́нут де́ло своё, кото́рое, в су́щности, почти́ ху́же безде́лья. Они́ чу́вствуют глубо́кое отвраще́ние от вся́кой форма́льности и, несмотря́ на то, — со́бственно потому́, что сми́рны, незлоби́вы и боя́тся, что́бы их не затро́нули, — са́ми пе́рвые формали́сты. Но до́ма они́ совсе́м в друго́м ви́де. Селя́тся они́ бо́льшею ча́стию в глубо́ком уедине́нии, по непристу́пным угла́м, как бу́дто тая́сь в них от люде́й и от све́та, и вообще́, да́же что́-то ме́лодрамати́ческое кида́ется в глаза́ при пе́рвом взгля́де на них. Они́ угрю́мы и неразгово́рчивы с дома́шними, углублены́ в себя́, но о́чень лю́бят все лени́вое, лёгкое, созерца́тельное, все де́йствующее не́жно на чу́вство и́ли возбужда́ющее ощуще́ния. Они́ лю́бят чита́ть, и чита́ть вся́кие кни́ги, да́же серьёзные, специа́льные, но обыкнове́нно со второ́й, тре́тьей страни́цы броса́ют чте́ние, и́бо удовлетвори́лись вполне́. Фанта́зия их, подви́жная, лету́чая, лёгкая, уже возбуждена́, впечатле́ние настро́ено, и це́лый мечта́тельный мир, с ра́достями, с го́рестями, с а́дом и ра́ем, с плени́тельнейшими же́нщинами, с геро́йскими по́двигами, с благоро́дною де́ятельностью, всегда́ с како́й-нибудь гига́нтской борьбо́ю, с преступле́ниями и вся́кими у́жасами, вдруг овладева́ет всем бытие́м мечта́теля. Ко́мната исчеза́ет, простра́нство то́же, вре́мя остана́вливается и́ли лети́т так бы́стро, что час идёт за мину́ту. Иногда́ це́лые но́чи прохо́дят незаме́тно в неопи́санных наслажде́ниях; ча́сто в не́сколько часо́в пережива́ется рай любви́ и́ли це́лая жизнь грома́дная, гига́нтская, неслы́ханная, чу́дная как сон, грандио́зно-прекра́сная. По како́му-то неве́домому произво́лу ускоря́ется пульс, бры́зжут слёзы, горя́т лихора́дочным огнём бле́дные, увлажнённые щёки и когда́ заря́ блеснёт свои́м ро́зовым све́том в око́шко мечта́теля, он бле́ден, бо́лен, исте́рзан и сча́стлив. Он броса́ется на посте́ль почти́ без па́мяти и, засыпа́я, ещё до́лго слы́шит боле́зненно-прия́тное, физи́ческое ощуще́ние в се́рдце... Мину́ты отрезвле́ния ужа́сны; несча́стный их не выно́сит и

pink in the dreamer's window, he is pale, ill, tormented, and happy. He throws himself into bed nearly unconscious and, as he falls asleep, he long continues to sense a painfully pleasurable physical feeling in his heart… The moments of sobering are awful; the unfortunate man cannot endure them and immediately takes his poison in new increased doses. Again the book, the musical motif, some old reminiscence from a faraway time, from real life, in a word, any one of thousands of reasons, the most insignificant, and the poison is ready, and again fantasy brilliantly, sumptuously spreads across an elaborate and fanciful canvas of quiet, impenetrable dreaming. He walks down the street with a hanging head, paying little attention to those around him, sometimes forgetting reality altogether, but if he does notice something, the most ordinary quotidian trifle, the most mundane, commonplace matter immediately takes on the hue of the fantastic. This is simply how his sight has been tuned, to see the fantastic in everything. Blinds drawn in the middle of the day, a hobbling old woman, a gentleman walking along waving his hands about as he pontificates to himself out loud – a sort, by the way, that one often encounters – a family scene through the window of a lowly little wooden hut – all that is almost always an adventure.

The imagination is tuned; an entire story, a novella, a novel is immediately born… On occasion, reality leaves a heavy, hostile impression on the heart of the dreamer, and he hastens to lose himself in his cherished, golden corner, which in actuality is often dusty, untidy, disordered, and dirty. Little by little, our trublemaker begins to shun crowds, shun common interests, and gradually, imperceptibly, any talent he may have for real life begins to dull. He naturally begins to feel that the pleasure his self-willed fantasy gives him is fuller, more sumptuous, and dearer than real life. Finally, in his delusion he absolutely loses the moral sense that enables a man to appreciate all the beauty of the real, he flounders, loses his bearings, misses moments of true happiness and languorously gives in to apathy and no longer wants to know that human life is a ceaseless self-contemplation in nature and in day-to-day life. Some dreamers even celebrate the anniversary of an experienced fantasy. They often notice the

немедленно принимает свой яд в новых увеличенных дозах. Опять-таки книга, музыкальный мотив, какое-нибудь воспоминание давнишнее, старое, из действительной жизни, одним словом, одна из тысяч причин, самых ничтожных, и яд готов, и снова фантазия ярко, роскошно раскидывается по узорчатой и прихотливой канве тихого, таинственного мечтания. На улице ходит повесив голову, мало обращая внимания на окружающих, иногда и тут совершенно забывая действительность но если заметит что, то самая обыкновенная житейская мелочь, самое пустое, обыденное дело немедленно принимает в нем колорит фантастический. Уж у него и взгляд так настроен, чтоб видеть во всем фантастическое. Затворённые ставни среди белого дня, исковерканная старуха, господин, идущий навстречу, размахивающий руками и рассуждающий вслух про себя, каких, между прочим, так много встречается, семейная картина в окне бедного деревянного домика — все это уже почти приключения.

Воображение настроено; тотчас рождается целая история, повесть, роман... Нередко же действительность производит впечатление тяжёлое, враждебное на сердце мечтателя, и он спешит забиться в свой заветный, золотой уголок, который на самом деле часто запылён, неопрятен, беспорядочен, грязен. Мало-помалу проказник наш начинает чуждаться толпы, чуждаться общих интересов, и постепенно, неприметно, начинает в нем притупляться талант действительной жизни. Ему естественно начинает казаться, что наслаждения, доставляемые его своевольной фантазиею, полнее, роскошнее, любовнее настоящей жизни. Наконец, в заблуждении своём он совершенно теряет то нравственное чутьё, которым человек способен оценить всю красоту настоящего, он сбивается, теряется, упускает моменты действительного счастья и, в апатии, лениво складывает руки и не хочет знать, что жизнь человеческая есть беспрерывное самосозерцание в природе и в насущной действительности. Бывают мечтатели, которые даже справляют годовщину своим фантастическим ощущениям. Они часто замечают числа месяцев, когда были особенно счастливы и когда их фантазия играла наиболее приятнейшим образом, и если бродили тогда в такой-то улице или читали такую-то книгу, видели

day of the month when they were especially happy and when the play of their fancy was particularly pleasant, and if they had been wandering at that time on a particular street or reading a particular book, or saw a particular woman, they will without fail try to repeat that particular experience on the anniversary of their impressions, copying and recalling the most minute circumstances of their putrid, feeble happiness. Is such a life not a tragedy! Is it not a sin and a horror! A caricature! And are we not all dreamers to a greater or lesser extent!...

Translation by Nora Favorov

такýю-то жéнщину, то уж непремéнно старáются повторúть то же сáамое и в годовщúну своúх впечатлéний, копúруя и припоминáя малéйшие обстоя́тельства своегó гнилóго, бессúльного счáстья. И не трагéдия такáя жизнь! Не грéх и не ýжас! Не карикатýра! И не все мы бóлее úли мéнее мечтáтели!..

Woodcut Portrait
Vladimir Favorsky, 1929

Letter Before Exile
Fyodor Dostoyevsky

In 1849 Dostoyevsky, alongside a number of friends and colleagues, was sentenced to death for participating in a radical discussion group, the Petrashevsky Circle. The pre-execution rituals were carried out, and Dostoyevsky was waiting to be taken to the scaffold when it was announced that the sentences were to be commuted to terms of hard labor. Both this incident, and the four years he then served in the prison camp at Omsk, had a profound effect on Dostoyevsky, leading to what he described as the "rebirth of my convictions" and the transformation of his view of the Russian peasantry. These experiences also left their mark on his writing, from the fictionalized memoir of his imprisonment in *Notes from the House of the Dead,* to the stories of execution told by Prince Myshkin in *The Idiot.* Dostoyevsky wrote this letter to his brother immediately before his transport to Siberia, and it is a remarkable expression of his sense of hope despite the trials he was about to face.

To M. M. Dostoyevsky
December 22, 1849, Peter and Paul Fortress, St. Petersburg

My good brother and friend! It's settled! I've been sentenced to four years of labor at a fortress (Orenburg, I think) and then service in the ranks. Today, the 22nd of December, we were brought to Semyonovsky Square. There, they read us all our death sentences, allowed us to kiss the cross, broke sabers over our heads, and dressed us for death (white shirts). Then three men were tied to stakes for the execution. I was sixth in line and they called three at a time, so I was in the second group and had no more than a minute to live. I thought of you, brother, and of yours. During that final minute you and you alone were in my thoughts. It was only then that I realized how much I love you, my darling brother! I also had time to embrace Pleshcheyev and Durov, who were nearby, and say farewell to them. Finally they sounded a retreat and those tied to the stake were brought back and they read to us that his imperial majesty was granting us life. This was followed by our actual sentences. Only Palm was acquitted. He was sent back to the army with the same rank.

Now they've told me, my good brother, that today or tomorrow we'll start our march. I asked to see you. But they told me that was impossible; I was only able to write you this letter, so you should also hurry and reply

М. М. ДОСТОЕВСКОМУ

22 декабря 1849. Петербург. Петропавловская крепость

Брат, любезный друг мой! всё решено! Я приговорён к 4-х летним работам в крепости (кажется, Оренбургской) и потом в рядовые. Сегодня 22 декабря нас отвезли на Семёновский плац. Там всем нам прочли смертный приговор, дали приложиться к кресту, переломили над головою шпаги и устроили наш предсмертный туалет (белые рубахи). Затем троих поставили к столбу для исполнения казни. Я стоял шестым, вызывали по трое, след<овательно>, я был во второй очереди и жить мне оставалось не более минуты. Я вспомнил тебя, брат, всех твоих; в последнюю минуту ты, только один ты, был в уме моем, я тут только узнал, как люблю тебя, брат мой милый! Я успел тоже обнять Плещеева, Дурова, которые были возле, и проститься с ними. Наконец ударили отбой, привязанных к столбу привели назад, и нам прочли, что его императорское величество дарует нам жизнь. Затем последовали настоящие приговоры. Один Пальм прощён. Его тем же чином в армию.

Сейчас мне сказали, любезный брат, что нам сегодня или завтра отправляться в поход. Я просил видеться с тобой. Но мне сказали, что это невозможно; могу только я тебе написать это письмо, по которому поторопись и ты дать мне поскорее отзыв. Я боюсь, что тебе как-нибудь

as soon as possible. I worry that you were somehow told of our sentence (to death). From the wagon's windows, when they were transporting us to Semyonovsky Square, I saw swarms of people; perhaps news had already reached you as well, and you were suffering on my account. Now you will be relieved. Brother! I am not gloomy and have not lost heart. Life is life wherever one might be, life is on the inside, not the outside. There will be people around me, and to be *a person* among people and always remain so, whatever misfortunes may come, not to despair or falter – that is what life is about, that is its purpose. I realize that now. This idea has become a part of me. It's true! The head that created, that lived the elevated life of art, that knew and grew accustomed to the lofty needs of the mind, that head has now been severed from my shoulders. What remains are memory and images that I have created but not yet brought to life. They will eat away at me, truly! But I still have a heart, and that same flesh and blood just as capable of loving, suffering, desiring, and remembering – and that is also life! *On voit le soleil!*

[…] Can it really be that I will never again take a pen in my hand? I think it may be possible in 4 years. I will send you everything that I write, if I write anything. My God! How many images lived and freshly created will perish, expire in my head or stream in my blood like a poison! Yes, if I cannot write I will perish. Better fifteen years imprisonment but with a pen in my hand.

[…] After all, I paid death a visit today, for three quarters of an hour I lived with that thought, I reached the final instant and now I am alive again!

[…] Life is a gift, life is happiness, every minute can be a century of happiness. *Si jeunesse savait!* Now that I've been given a different life, I am reborn in a new form. Brother! I swear to you that I will not lose hope and will keep my spirit and heart pure. I will be reborn for the better. This is my sole hope, my sole consolation…

Translation by Nora Favorov

был изве́стен наш пригово́р (к сме́рти). Из о́кон каре́ты, когда́ везли́ на Семён<овский> плац, я ви́дел бе́здну наро́да; мо́жет быть, ве́сть уже́ прошла́ и до тебя́, и ты страда́л за меня́. Тепе́рь тебе́ бу́дет ле́гче за меня́. Брат! я не уны́л и не упа́л ду́хом. Жизнь везде́ жизнь, жизнь в нас сами́х, а не во вне́шнем. По́дле меня́ бу́дут лю́ди, и быть челове́ком ме́жду людьми́ и оста́ться им навсегда́, в каки́х бы то ни́ было несча́стьях, не уны́ть и не па́сть — вот в чём жизнь, в чём зада́ча её. Я созна́л э́то. Э́та иде́я вошла́ в пло́ть и кро́вь мою́. Да, пра́вда! та голова́, кото́рая создава́ла, жила́ вы́сшею жи́знию иску́сства, кото́рая созна́ла и свы́клась с возвы́шенными потре́бностями ду́ха, та голова́ уже́ сре́зана с плеч мои́х. Оста́лась па́мять и о́бразы, со́зданные и ещё не воплощённые мной. Они́ изъязвя́т меня́, пра́вда! Но во мне оста́лось се́рдце и та же пло́ть и кро́вь, кото́рая та́кже мо́жет и люби́ть, и страда́ть, и жела́ть, и по́мнить, а э́то всё-таки жизнь! On voit le soleil!

[…] Неуже́ли никогда́ я не возьму́ пера́ в руки? Я ду́маю, че́рез 4-ре го́да бу́дет возмо́жно. Я перешлю́ тебе́ всё, что напишу́, е́сли что-нибу́дь напишу́. Бо́же мой! Ско́лько о́бразов, вы́житых, со́зданных мно́ю вновь, поги́бнет, уга́снет в мое́й голове́ и́ли отра́вой в крови́ разольётся! Да, е́сли нельзя́ бу́дет писа́ть, я поги́бну. Лу́чше пятна́дцать лет заключе́ния и перо́ в рука́х.

[…] Ведь был же я сего́дня у сме́рти, три че́тверти ча́са прожи́л с э́той мы́слию, был у после́днего мгнове́ния и тепе́рь ещё раз живу́!

[…] Жизнь — дар, жизнь — сча́стье, ка́ждая мину́та могла́ быть ве́ком сча́стья. Si jeunesse savait! Тепе́рь, переменя́я жизнь, перерожда́юсь в но́вую фо́рму. Брат! Кляну́сь тебе́, что я не потеря́ю наде́жду и сохраню́ дух мой и се́рдце в чистоте́. Я перерожу́сь к лу́чшему. Вот вся наде́жда моя́, всё утеше́ние моё. …

Fyodor Dostoyevsky, 1860

Masha is Lying on the Table
Fyodor Dostoyevsky

In 1864 Dostoyevsky wrote *Notes from Underground,* which became one of his most famous and influential works, but this was also a painful year personally and professionally, as he faced the deaths of his first wife, Maria (Masha), and his beloved brother, Mikhail, as well as the collapse of the journal the brothers had edited, *The Epoch,* because of excessive debts. Dostoyevsky's marriage to Maria Isayeva, a widow he met whilst in exile in Semipalatinsk following his prison sentence, was a difficult one. She suffered from tuberculosis, which made her increasingly mentally unstable in the final years of her life, and Dostoyevsky conducted a tempestuous and obsessive affair with Apollinaria Suslova during this period. Nevertheless, immediately following his wife's death, Dostoyevsky wrote the entry in his private diary known as "Masha is lying on the table," an extraordinary and impassioned meditation on death, immortality and human relationships. One of the frankest expressions of his developing religious faith, it provides a fascinating insight into the spiritual dimension of his novels.

II. NOTEBOOK, 1863-1864

April 16. Masha is lying on the table. Will I see Masha again?

To love another *as yourself,* in accordance with the teachings of Christ, is impossible. The earthly law of the self ties you down. The *I* hinders you. Only Christ was capable of this, but Christ was an eternal, timeless ideal, toward which man strives and, by natural law, must strive. All the same, after the appearance of Christ *as the human ideal in the flesh*, it became clear as day that the greatest and final evolution of the self must, after all, lead to (at the very end of its development, at the very point of achieving its end) man finding, realizing, and becoming convinced, with the full force of his nature, that the greatest use to which man can put his self and the full development of his I is to destroy that I, to give all of it away to each and every person, completely and unconditionally. And that is the greatest joy. Thus, the law of the self fuses with humanist law, and in this fusion, both *I* and *everyone* (apparently, two extremes), which are mutually destroyed for each other's sake, at the same time attain the highest aim of their individual evolutions, each one separately.

This is truly Christ's paradise. All history, both of mankind and, in part, of each person individually, is merely development, struggle, pursuit, and the achievement of this end.

II. ЗАПИСНА́Я КНИ́ЖКА 1863-1864 гг.

16 апре́ля. Ма́ша лежи́т на столе́. Уви́жусь ли с Ма́шей?

Возлюби́ть челове́ка, как самого́ себя́, по за́поведи Христо́вой, — невозмо́жно. Зако́н ли́чности на земле́ свя́зывает. Я препя́тствует. Оди́н Христо́с мог, но Христо́с был векове́чный от ве́ка идеа́л, к кото́рому стреми́тся и по зако́ну приро́ды до́лжен стреми́ться челове́к. Ме́жду те́м по́сле появле́ния Христа́, как идеа́ла челове́ка во плоти́, ста́ло я́сно как день, что высоча́йшее, после́днее разви́тие ли́чности и́менно и должно́ дойти́ до того́ (в са́мом конце́ разви́тия, в са́мом пу́нкте достиже́ния це́ли), чтоб челове́к нашёл, созна́л и всей си́лой свое́й приро́ды убеди́лся, что высоча́йшее употребле́ние, кото́рое мо́жет сде́лать челове́к из свое́й ли́чности, из полноты́ разви́тия своего́ я, — э́то как бы уничто́жить э́то я, отда́ть его́ целико́м всем и ка́ждому безразде́льно и беззаве́тно. И э́то велича́йшее сча́стие. Таки́м о́бразом, зако́н я слива́ется с зако́ном гумани́зма, и в сли́тии, о́ба, и я и всё (по-ви́димому, две кра́йние противоположности), взаи́мно уничто́ж<енн>ые друг для дру́га, в то же са́мое вре́мя достига́ют и вы́сшей цели своего́ индивидуа́льного разви́тия ка́ждый осо́бо.

Э́то-то и е́сть рай Христо́в. Вся исто́рия, как челове́чества, так отча́сти и ка́ждого отде́льно, есть то́лько разви́тие, борьба́, стремле́ние и достиже́ние э́той це́ли.

But if this is the final goal of mankind (having achieved which man will not need to develop, that is, to attain, struggle, perceive the ideal despite all his failures, and strive ever towards it – meaning, he will not need to live), then it follows that man, by achieving, ends his earthly existence. Thus, man on Earth is merely a developing being, and therefore he is not complete, but transitional.

But achieving such a great aim, as I see it, is completely pointless if upon the achievement of the aim all fades and disappears; that is, if man is to have no life even once he achieves the aim. Ergo, there exists a future, heavenly life.

What is it, where is it, on what planet, in what center – that is, in the final center, meaning the bosom of universal synthesis, that is, in God? – we do not know. We know only one trait of the future nature of this future being, which is unlikely to even be called human (consequently, we have absolutely no idea what kinds of beings we will be). This trait has been anticipated and predicted by Christ – that great and final ideal of all of mankind's development, who appeared before us, according to the law of our history, in the flesh; and that trait was:

"They neither marry nor lay claims, but are as angels of God." A deeply significant trait.

1) They neither *marry* nor *lay claims* – as there is no need: it is no longer necessary to develop, to attain the end through generational change, and

2) Marriage and laying claim to a woman are, to a certain extent, the greatest rejection of humanism, the complete detachment of a couple from *everyone else* (very little is left for everyone else). Family – that is, a law of nature – is, for man, nonetheless an abnormal and selfish state, in the fullest sense of the word. Family is the holiest thing man has on Earth, for through this law of nature man achieves a development (that is, generational change) in his purpose. But at the same time, also as a law of nature, for the sake of his goal's final ideal, man must incessantly deny his family. (Duality).

Но е́сли э́то цель оконча́тельная челове́чества (дости́гнув кото́рой ему́ не на́до бу́дет развива́ться, то́ есть достига́ть, боро́ться, прозрева́ть при всех паде́ниях свои́х идеа́л и ве́чно стреми́ться к нему́, — ста́ло быть, не на́до бу́дет жить) — то, сле́дственно, челове́к, достига́я, око́нчивает своё земно́е существова́ние. Ита́к, челове́к есть на земле́ существо́ то́лько развива́ющееся, сле́довательно, не око́нченное, а перехо́дное.

Но достига́ть тако́й вели́кой це́ли, по моему́ рассужде́нию, соверше́нно бессмы́сленно, е́сли при достиже́нии це́ли всё угаса́ет и исчеза́ет, то́ есть е́сли не бу́дет жи́зни у челове́ка и по достиже́нии це́ли. Сле́дственно, есть бу́дущая, ра́йская жизнь.

Кака́я она́, где она́, на како́й плане́те, в како́м це́нтре, в оконча́тельном ли це́нтре, то́ есть в ло́не всео́бщего си́нтеза, то́ есть бо́га? — мы не зна́ем. Мы зна́ем то́лько одну́ черту́ бу́дущей приро́ды бу́дущего существа́, кото́рое вря́д ли бу́дет и называ́ться челове́ком (след<овательно>, и поня́тия мы не име́ем, каки́ми бу́дем мы существа́ми). Эта черта предска́зана и предуга́дана Христо́м, — вели́ким и коне́чным идеа́лом разви́тия всего́ челове́чества, — предста́вшим нам, по зако́ну на́шей исто́рии, во плоти́; э́та че́рта:

«Не же́нятся и не посяга́ют, а живу́т, как а́нгелы бо́жии». — Че́рта глубоко знамена́тельная.

1) Не же́нятся и не посяга́ют, — и́бо не́ для чего́; развива́ться, достига́ть це́ли, посре́дством сме́ны поколе́ний уже́ не на́до и

2) Жени́тьба и посягнове́ние на же́нщину есть как бы велича́йшее оттолкнове́ние от гумани́зма, соверше́нное обособле́ние па́ры от всех (ма́ло остаётся для всех). Семе́йство, то́ есть зако́н приро́ды, но всё-таки ненорма́льное, эгоисти́ческое в по́лном смы́сле состоя́ние от челове́ка. Семе́йство — э́то велича́йшая святы́ня челове́ка на земле́, и́бо посре́дством э́того зако́на приро́ды челове́к достига́ет разви́тия (то́ есть сме́ной поколе́ний) це́ли. Но в то же вре́мя челове́к по зако́ну же приро́ды, во и́мя оконча́тельного идеа́ла свое́й це́ли, до́лжен беспреры́вно отрица́ть его́. (Дво́йственность).

NB. Antichrists are wrong in trying to refute Christianity by using the following central counterpoint: 1) "Why does Christianity not reign on Earth, if it is the true faith; why does man still suffer, rather than becoming a brother to his fellow man?"

Oh, but the answer is so clear: because this is the ideal of man's future, final life, whereas on Earth man exists in a transitional state. It will happen, but only after the achievement of the goal, when man will be completely reborn, according to the laws of nature, into another form, which will neither marry nor lay claims. And a 2nd point. Christ himself professed his teaching only as an ideal and predicted that before the end of the world there would be struggle and evolution (the teaching of the sword), for such is the law of nature, because on Earth life is evolutionary, while there it will be a synthetically complete existence, eternally full and jubilant, for which, then, "time will be no more."

NB2. Atheists, who deny the existence of God and the afterlife, are horrifically prone to conceptualizing it all in a human form – therein lies their sin. The nature of God is the polar opposite to that of man. Man, through the great results of science, moves from multiplicity to Synthesis, from facts to their generalization and understanding. But God's nature is different. It is the complete synthesis of all existence, which regards itself in multiplicity, in Analysis.

But if man will not be man – what will his nature be?

On Earth this is beyond understanding, but its law may be forefelt, both by all mankind in direct emanations (Proudhon, the origin of God) and by each individual.

This is a fusion of the complete self, that is, of knowledge and synthesis, *with everything. "Love everything as yourself."* This is impossible on Earth, as it contradicts the law of individual development and the achievement of the final goal, by which man is bound. Consequently, this is not the ideal law, as the Antichrists say, but the law of our ideal.

NB. Антихристы ошибаются, опровергая христианство следующим главным пунктом опровержения: 1) «Отчего же христианство не царит на земле, если оно истинно; отчего же человек до сих пор страдает, а не делается братом друг другу?»

Да очень понятно почему: потому что это идеал будущей, окончательной жизни человека, а на земле человек в состоянии переходном. Это будет, но будет после достижения цели, когда человек переродится по законам природы окончательно в другую натуру, которая не женится и не посягает, и, 2-е. Сам Христос проповедовал своё учение только как идеал, сам предрёк, что до конца мира будет борьба и развитие (учение о мече), ибо это закон природы, потому что на земле жизнь развивающаяся, а там — бытие, полное синтетически, вечно наслаждающееся и наполненное, для которого, стало быть, «времени больше не будет».

NB2. Атеисты, отрицающие бога и будущую жизнь, ужасно наклонны представлять всё это в человеческом виде, тем и грешат. Натура бога прямо противоположна натуре человека. Человек по великому результату науки, идёт от многоразличия к Синтезу, от фактов к обобщению их и познанию. А натура бога другая. Это полный синтез всего бытия, саморассматривающий себя в многоразличии, в Анализе.

Но если человек не человек — какова же будет его природа?

Понять нельзя на земле, но закон её может предчувствоваться и всем человечеством в непосредственных эманациях (Прудон, происхождение бога) и каждым частным лицом.

Это слитие полного я, то есть знания и синтеза со всем. «Возлюби всё, как себя.» это на земле невозможно, ибо противуречит закону развития личности и достижения окончательной цели, которым связан человек. Следовательно, это закон не идеальный, как говорят антихристы, а нашего идеала.

NB. Thus, all depends on whether or not one accepts Christ as the final earthly ideal; that is, it depends on the Christian faith. If you believe in Christ, then you also believe that you will live forever.

Is there, then, an afterlife for any given *I*? It is said that man breaks down and dies *completely*.

We already have reason to doubt this completeness because as one who physically begets a son transfers to him a part of his identity, so in moral terms man leaves his memory to other people (NB. the *Memory Eternal prayer* at funeral services is significant), meaning that he enters into mankind's future development through a part of his previous, Earth-abiding self. We can clearly see that the memory of the great developers of mankind lives among men (as does the development of miscreants), and resembling them is man's great joy. This means that part of these personalities enters into other people, in both flesh and soul. Christ fully entered into mankind, and man strives to transform into Christ, as his ideal. Having achieved this, he will clearly see that everyone who achieved the same aim on Earth also entered into the composition of his final identity – meaning Christ. (Christ's synthetic nature is amazing. For it is the nature of God, which means that Christ is the reflection of God on Earth.) It is hard to imagine the resurrection of each individual *I* in that moment, in the general Synthesis. But that which lives, that which did not die even up to the very attainment, and which was reflected in the final ideal, must come alive in the final, synthetic, eternal life. We will become faces, never ceasing our fusion with everything, neither marrying nor laying claims, and remaining in various ranks (my Father's house has many rooms). All will then feel and know itself forever. But how that will be, in what form, and of what nature – it is difficult for man to even imagine it fully.

Thus, while on Earth man strives for an ideal *in opposition* to his nature. When man has not fulfilled the law of striving for the ideal, that is, when he has not, through love, sacrificed his *I* to all people or to another being (as I with Masha), he experiences suffering and calls that state "sin."

NB. Ита́к, всё зави́сит от того́: принима́ется ли Христо́с за оконча́тельный идеа́л на земле́, то́ есть от ве́ры христиа́нской. Ко́ли ве́ришь во Христа́, то ве́ришь, что и жить бу́дешь вове́ки.

Есть ли в тако́м слу́чае бу́дущая жизнь для вся́кого я? Говоря́т, челове́к разруша́ется и умира́ет весь.

Мы уже́ потому́ зна́ем, что не весь, что челове́к, как физи́чески рожда́ющий сы́на, передаёт ему́ часть свое́й ли́чности, та́к и нра́вственно оставля́ет па́мять свою́ лю́дям (NB. Пожела́ние ве́чной па́мяти на панихи́дах знамена́тельно), то́ есть вхо́дит ча́стию свое́й пре́жней, жи́вшей на земле́ ли́чности, в бу́дущее разви́тие челове́чества. Мы нагля́дно ви́дим, что па́мять вели́ких развива́телей челове́ка живёт ме́жду людьми́ (ра́вно как и злоде́ев разви́тие), и да́же для челове́ка велича́йшее сча́стье походи́ть на них. Зна́чит, часть э́тих нату́р вхо́дит и пло́тью и одушевлённо в други́х люде́й. Христо́с весь вошёл в челове́чество, и челове́к стреми́тся преобрази́ться в Христа́ как в свой идеа́л. Дости́гнув э́того, он я́сно уви́дит, что и всё, достига́вшие на земле́ э́той же це́ли, вошли́ в соста́в его́ оконча́тельной нату́ры, то́ есть в Христа́. (Синтети́ческая нату́ра Христа́ изуми́тельна. Ведь э́то нату́ра бо́га, зна́чит, Христо́с есть отраже́ние бо́га на земле́.) Как воскре́снет тогда́ ка́ждое я — в о́бщем Си́нтезе — тру́дно предста́вить. Но живо́е, не у́мершее да́же до самого́ достиже́ния и отрази́вшееся в оконча́тельном идеа́ле — должно́ ожи́ть в жизнь оконча́тельную, синтети́ческую, бесконе́чную. Мы бу́дем — ли́ца, не перестава́я слива́ться со всем, не посяга́я и не женя́сь, и в разли́чных разря́дах (в дому́ отца́ моего́ оби́тели мно́ги су́ть). Всё себя́ тогда́ почу́вствует и позна́ет наве́чно. Но как э́то бу́дет, в како́й фо́рме, в како́й приро́де, — челове́ку тру́дно и предста́вить себе́ оконча́тельно.

Ита́к, челове́к стреми́тся на земле́ к идеа́лу, противуполо́жному его́ нату́ре. Когда́ челове́к не испо́лнил зако́на стремле́ния к идеа́лу, то́ есть не приноси́л любо́вью в же́ртву своего́ я лю́дям и́ли друго́му существу́ (я и Ма́ша), он чу́вствует страда́ние и назва́л э́то состоя́ние грехо́м.

Thus, man must constantly experience suffering, which is balanced out by the heavenly pleasure of fulfilling the law – the sacrifice. In that lies the earthly balance. Otherwise Earth would be without purpose.

The materialist teaching is one of universal inertness and the mechanics of matter, meaning death. The teaching of true philosophy is the destruction of inertness – meaning thought, that is, the center and Synthesis of the universe – and of matter, its external form – meaning God, meaning eternal life.

The confusion and uncertainty of today's conceptions can be explained quite simply: it happens, in part, because the proper study of nature has not been going on for very long (Descartes, Bacon), and because the facts we have gathered are as of yet *extremely* insufficient to derive any conclusions whatsoever. And yet we rush to make such conclusions, obeying our developmental law. As for deriving final results from current facts and being *content* with them, only the most limited minds are capable of doing so, no matter who they are and what they call themselves.

The problem with a revolutionary party is that it will produce more racket than the result is worth and spill far more blood than all the benefits achieved are worth. (Then again, they think blood cheap.) Any given society can only accommodate the particular level of progress up to which it has developed and which it has begun to understand. So why reach further, why all the way to the moon? That can ruin everything, because you might frighten everybody. In '48, even the bourgeois agreed to demand rights, but when they were about to be led further, to where they could not understand (and where it was really quite stupid to go), they began to fight back and won. Currently, Europe may only need some more self-rule and more freedom of the press. But they cannot even achieve *that* over there. Society is suspicious and in no state to endure freedom. All the blood of revolutionary dreams, all the uproar and underground activity will lead nowhere and come crashing down on their own heads.

Ита́к, челове́к беспреры́вно до́лжен чу́вствовать страда́ние, кото́рое уравнове́шивается ра́йским наслажде́нием исполне́ния зако́на, то́ есть же́ртвой. Тут-то и равнове́сие земно́е. Ина́че земля́ была́ бы бессмы́сленна.

Уче́ние материали́стов — всео́бщая ко́сность и механи́зм вещества́, зна́чит смерть. Уче́ние и́стинной филосо́фии — уничтоже́ние ко́сности, то́ есть мысль, то́ есть центр и Си́нтез вселе́нной и нару́жной фо́рмы её — вещества́, то́ есть бог, то́ есть жизнь бесконе́чная.

Пу́таница и неопределённость тепе́решних поня́тий происхо́дит по са́мой просте́йшей причи́не: отча́сти оттого́, что пра́вильное изуче́ние приро́ды происхо́дит весьма́ неда́вно (Дека́рт и Бэ́кон) и что мы ещё собра́ли до кра́йности ма́ло фа́ктов, чтоб вы́вести из них хоть каки́е-нибу́дь заключе́ния. А ме́жду те́м торо́пимся де́лать э́ти заключе́ния, повину́ясь на́шему зако́ну разви́тия. Выводи́ть же оконча́тельные результа́ты из тепе́решних фа́ктов и успоко́иваться на э́том мо́гут ра́зве то́лько са́мые ограни́ченные нату́ры, кто бы они́ ни бы́ли и как бы ни называ́лись.

Революцио́нная па́ртия тем дурна́, что нагреми́т бо́льше, чем результа́т сто́ит, нальёт крови́ гора́здо бо́льше, чем сто́ит вся полу́ченная вы́года. (Впро́чем, кро́вь у них дешева́.) Вся́кое о́бщество мо́жет вмести́ть то́лько ту сте́пень прогре́сса, до кото́рой оно́ доразви́лось и начало́ понима́ть. К чему́ же хва<та́>ть да́льше, с не́ба-то звёзды? э́тим всё мо́жно погуби́ть, потому́ что всех мо́жно испуга́ть. В со́рок восьмо́м да́же буржуа́ согласи́лся тре́бовать прав, но когда́ его́ напра́вили бы́ло да́льше, где он ничего́ поня́ть не мог (и где в са́мом де́ле бы́ло глу́по), то он на́чал отбива́ться и победи́л. В настоя́щее вре́мя в Евро́пе ну́жно то́лько возмо́жно бо́льше самоуправле́ния и свобо́ды пре́ссы. Но там и э́то не дости́гнешь. о́бщество подозри́тельно и не в состоя́нии вы́несть свобо́ды. Вся э́та кровь, кото́рою бре́дят революционе́ры, весь э́тот гвалт и вся э́та подзе́мная рабо́та ни к чему́ не приведу́т и на их же го́ловы обру́шатся.

By freeing the serfs in Poland and granting them land, Russia has already given Poland some of her thought, inculcated Poland with her character, and that thought is the *chain* that now binds Poland and Russia inseparably.

Return to the soil.

No one can *be* anything or *achieve* anything without first being himself.

Translation by Eugenia Sokolskaya

Освобожда́я в По́льше крестья́н и уделя́я им зе́млю, Росси́я уж удели́ла По́льше свою́ мысль, приви́ла ей свой хара́ктер, и э́та мысль — цепь, с кото́рою тепе́рь По́льша с Росси́ею свя́зана разде́льно.

Вороти́ться к по́чве.

Никто́ не мо́жет быть чем-нибу́дь и́ли достигнуть чего́-нибу́дь, не быв снача́ла сами́м собо́ю.

St. Petersburg Passazh

The Crocodile
An Extraordinary Incident, or the Passage in the Passazh

Fyodor Dostoyevsky

Written in 1865, between the publication of *Notes from Underground* and *Crime and Punishment,* "The Crocodile" is one of Dostoyevsky's funniest stories. A brilliant satire on political economy and the importation of Western ideas onto Russian soil, it is also a strong indication of the central role money plays in his fiction. Although Dostoyevsky denied the connection, the philosophical spoutings of the mediocre Ivan Matveich from inside the crocodile have been viewed as parody of the imprisoned radical Nikolai Chernyshevsky, whose utopian novel *What is to be Done?* was subject to Dostoyevsky's attack in *Notes from Underground.* The setting of "The Crocodile," in Petersburg's fashionable "Passazh" Arcade off Nevsky Prospect, can be interpreted as a consumerist version of the Crystal Palace that houses the perfect future society in Chernyshevsky's work. Dostoyevsky's reputation suffered after the October 1917 revolution because of his rejection of revolutionary doctrines, but "The Crocodile" gave its name to a highly popular satirical magazine founded in 1922 in the Soviet Union.

A true story of how a gentleman of a certain age and of reputable appearance was swallowed alive and whole by the crocodile in the Passazh, and of the consequences that followed.

Ohe Lambert! Ou est Lambert? As-tu vu Lambert?

I

On the thirteenth of January of this present year, 1865, at half-past midday, Elena Ivanovna, the wife of my educated friend Ivan Matveich [...] expressed the desire to see the crocodile now on view at a fixed charge in the Passazh. As Ivan Matveich had already in his pocket his ticket for a tour abroad (not so much for his health as from intellectual curiosity), and was consequently free from his official duties and had nothing whatever to do that morning, he offered no objection to his wife's irresistible fancy, but was positively aflame with curiosity himself. "A capital idea!" he said, with the utmost satisfaction. "We'll have a look at the crocodile! On the eve of visiting Europe it's as well to acquaint ourselves on the spot with its indigenous inhabitants." And with these words, taking his wife's arm, he set off with her at once for the Passazh. I joined them, as I usually do, being an intimate friend of the family. I have never seen Ivan Matveich in a more agreeable frame of mind than he was on that memorable morning [...]. On

Справедли́вая по́весть о том, как оди́н господи́н, изве́стных лет и изве́стной нару́жности, пасса́жным крокоди́лом был прогло́чен живьём, весь без оста́тка, и что из э́того вы́шло.

Ohé Lambert! Oú est Lambert? As-tu vu Lambert?

I

Сего́ трина́дцатого января́ теку́щего шестьдеся́т пя́того го́да, в полови́не пе́рвого пополу́дни, Еле́на Ива́новна, супру́га Ива́на Матве́ича [...] пожела́ла посмотре́ть крокоди́ла, пока́зываемого за изве́стную пла́ту в Пасса́же. Име́я уже́ в карма́не сво́й биле́т для вы́езда (не сто́лько по боле́зни, ско́лько из любозна́тельности) за грани́цу, — а сле́дственно, уже́ счита́ясь по слу́жбе в о́тпуску и, ста́ло быть, бу́дучи соверше́нно в то у́тро свобо́ден, Ива́н Матве́ич не то́лько не воспрепя́тствовал непреодоли́мому жела́нию свое́й супру́ги, но да́же сам возгоре́лся любопы́тством. «Прекра́сная иде́я, — сказа́л он вседово́льно, — осмо́трим крокоди́ла! Собира́ясь в Евро́пу, не ху́до познако́миться ещё на ме́сте с населя́ющими её тузе́мцами», — и с си́ми слова́ми, приня́в под ру́чку свою́ супру́гу, тотча́с же отпра́вился с не́ю в Пасса́ж. Я же, по обыкнове́нию моему́, увяза́лся с ни́ми ря́дом — в ви́де дома́шнего дру́га. Никогда́ ещё я не ви́дел Ива́на Матве́ича в бо́лее прия́тном расположе́нии ду́ха, как в то па́мятное для меня́ у́тро

entering the Passazh he was at once full of admiration for the splendours of the building and, when we reached the shop in which the monster lately arrived in Petersburg was being exhibited, he volunteered to pay the quarter-ruble for me to the crocodile owner – something which had never happened before. Walking into a little room, we observed that besides the crocodile there were parrots of the foreign species known as cockatoo, as well as a group of monkeys in a special case in a recess. Near the entrance, along the left wall stood a big tin tank that looked like a bath covered with a solid iron grating, filled with water to the depth of two inches. In this shallow pool was kept a huge crocodile, which lay like a log absolutely motionless and apparently deprived of all its faculties by our damp climate, so inhospitable to foreign visitors. [...]

"So this is the crocodile!" said Elena Ivanovna, with a pathetic cadence of regret. [...]

The owner of the crocodile, a German, came out and looked at us with an air of extraordinary pride.

"He has a right to be," Ivan Matveich whispered to me, "he knows he's the only man in Russia exhibiting a crocodile." [...]

"I fancy your crocodile is not alive," said Elena Ivanovna, piqued by the recalcitrance of the proprietor [...].

"Oh, no, madam," the latter replied in broken Russian; and instantly moving the grating half off the tank, he poked the monster's head with a stick. Then the treacherous monster, to show it was alive, faintly stirred its paws and tail, raised its snout and emitted something like a prolonged snuffle. [...]

"How horrid that crocodile is! I'm really frightened," Elena Ivanovna twittered [...]. "Come, Semyon Semyonich," Elena Ivanovna continued, addressing me exclusively, "let's go and look at the monkeys. I'm awfully fond of monkeys; they're such darlings ... and the crocodile is horrid."

[...]. Войдя́ в Пасса́ж, он неме́дленно стал восхища́ться великоле́пием зда́ния, а подойдя́ к магази́ну, в кото́ром пока́зывалось вновь привезённое в столи́цу чудо́вище, сам пожела́л заплати́ть за меня́ четверта́к крокоди́льщику, чего́ пре́жде с ним никогда́ не случа́лось. Вступи́в в небольшу́ю ко́мнату, мы заме́тили, что в ней кро́ме крокоди́ла заключа́ются ещё попуга́и из иностра́нной поро́ды какаду́ и, сверх того́, гру́ппа обезья́н в осо́бом шкафу́ в углубле́ний. У самого́ же вхо́да, у ле́вой стены́ стоя́л большо́й жестяно́й я́щик в ви́де как бы ва́нны, накры́тый кре́пкою желе́зною се́ткой, а на дне его́ бы́ло на вершо́к воды́. В э́той-то мелково́дной лу́же сохраня́лся огро́мнейший крокоди́л, лежа́вший, как бревно́, совершён но без движе́ния и, ви́димо, лиши́вшийся всех свои́х спосо́бностей от на́шего сыро́го и негостеприи́много для иностра́нцев кли́мата. [...]

— Так э́то-то крокоди́л! — сказа́ла Еле́на Ива́новна го́лосом сожале́ния и нараспе́в. [...]

Вы́шедший к нам не́мец, хозя́ин, со́бственник крокоди́ла с чрезвыча́йно го́рдым ви́дом смотре́л на нас.

— Он прав, — шепну́л мне Ива́н Матве́ич, — и́бо созна́ет, что он оди́н во всей Росси́и пока́зывает тепе́рь крокоди́ла. [...]

— Мне ка́жется, ваш крокоди́л не живо́й, — проговори́ла опя́ть Еле́на Ива́новна, пикиро́ванная неподатливостью хозя́ина. [...]

— О нет, мада́м, — отвеча́л тот ло́маным ру́сским языко́м и тотча́с же, приподня́в до полови́ны се́тку я́щика, стал па́лочкой ты́кать крокоди́ла в го́лову.

Тогда́ кова́рное чудо́вище, чтоб показа́ть свои́ при́знаки жи́зни, слегка́ пошевели́ло ла́пами и хвосто́м, приподня́ло ры́ло и испусти́ло не́что подо́бное продолжи́тельному сопе́нью. [...]

— Како́й проти́вный э́тот крокоди́л! Я да́же испуга́лась, – [...] пролепета́ла Еле́на Ива́новна [...]. — Пойдёмте, Семён Семёныч, — продолжа́ла Еле́на Ива́новна, обраща́ясь исключи́тельно ко мне, — посмо́тримте лу́чше обезья́н. Я ужа́сно люблю́ обезья́н; из них таки́е ду́шки... а крокоди́л ужа́сен.

"Oh, don't be afraid, my dear!" Ivan Matveich called after us, gallantly displaying his manly courage to his wife. "This drowsy denizen of the realms of the Pharaohs will do us no harm." And he remained by the tank. What's more, he took his glove and began tickling the crocodile's nose with it, wishing, as he admitted afterwards, to make him snort again. [...]

And it was at that very moment that a terrible, I may say unnatural, scream shook the room. [...] I saw – oh, heavens! – I saw the luckless Ivan Matveich in the terrible jaws of the crocodile, held by them round the torso, lifted horizontally in the air and desperately kicking. [...] The crocodile began by turning the unhappy Ivan Matveich in his terrible jaws so that he could swallow his legs first; then bringing up Ivan Matveich, who kept trying to jump out and clutching at the sides of the tank, sucked him down again as far as his waist. [...] At last, with a final gulp, the crocodile swallowed my educated friend entirely, this time leaving no trace of him. From the outside of the crocodile we could see the whole of Ivan Matveich's figure as he passed down the inside of the monster. [...] The crocodile made a tremendous effort, probably oppressed by the magnitude of the object he had swallowed, once more opened his terrible chops, and with a final belch he suddenly let the head of Ivan Matveich pop out for a second [...]. It seemed as though that despairing countenance had only popped out to cast one last look on the objects around it, to take its last farewell of all earthly pleasures. But it had not time to carry out its intention; the crocodile made another effort, gave a gulp and instantly it vanished again – this time for ever. This appearance and disappearance of a still living human head was so horrible, but all the same [...] there was something so comic about it that I suddenly quite unexpectedly exploded with laughter. But pulling myself together and realising that to laugh at such a moment was not the thing for an old family friend, I turned at once to Elena Ivanovna and said with a sympathetic air:

"Now it's all over with our friend Ivan Matveich!"

— О, не бойся, друг мой, — прокричал нам вслед Иван Матвеич, приятно храбрясь перед своею супругою. — Этот сонливый обитатель фараонова царства ничего нам не сделает, — и остался у ящика. Мало того, взяв свою перчатку, он начал щекотать ею нос крокодила, желая, как признался он после, заставить его вновь сопеть. [...]

И вот в это-то самое мгновение вдруг страшный, могу даже сказать, неестественный крик потряс комнату. [...] Я увидел, — о боже! — я увидел несчастного Ивана Матвеича в ужасных челюстях крокодиловых, перехваченного ими поперёк туловища, уже поднятого горизонтально на воздух и отчаянно болтавшего в нем ногами. [...] Крокодил начал с того, что, повернув бедного Ивана Матвеича в своих ужасных челюстях к себе ногами, сперва проглотил самые ноги; потом, отрыгнув немного Ивана Матвеича, старавшегося выскочить и цеплявшегося руками за ящик, вновь втянул его в себя уже выше поясницы. [...] Наконец, глотнув окончательно, крокодил вобрал в себя всего моего образованного друга и на этот раз уже без остатка. На поверхности крокодила можно было заметить, как проходил по его внутренности Иван Матвеич со всеми своими формами. [...] крокодил понатужился, вероятно давясь от огромности проглоченного им предмета, снова раскрыл всю ужасную пасть свою, и из неё, в виде последней отрыжки, вдруг на одну секунду выскочила голова Ивана Матвеича [...]. Казалось, эта отчаянная голова для того только и выскочила, чтоб ещё раз бросить последний взгляд на все предметы и мысленно проститься со всеми светскими удовольствиями. Но она не успела в своём намерении: крокодил вновь собрался с силами, глотнул — и вмиг она снова исчезла, в этот раз уже навеки. Это появление и исчезновение ещё живой человеческой головы было так ужасно, но вместе с тем [...] заключало в себе что-то до того смешное, что я вдруг и совсем неожиданно фыркнул; но, спохватившись, что смеяться в такую минуту мне в качестве домашнего друга неприлично, обратился тотчас же к Елене Ивановне и с симпатическим видом сказал ей:

— Теперь капут нашему Ивану Матвеичу!

I cannot even attempt to describe how violent was the agitation of Elena Ivanovna during the whole process. After the first scream she seemed rooted to the spot, and stared at the catastrophe with apparent indifference [...]; then she suddenly went off into a heart-rending wail [...].

At this instant the proprietor, too, who had at first been also petrified by horror, suddenly threw up his hands and cried, gazing to the heavens: "Oh, my crocodile! *Oh, mein allerliebster Karlchen! Mutter, Mutter, Mutter!*"

A door at the rear of the room opened at this cry, and the Mutter, a rosy-cheeked, elderly but dishevelled woman in a cap, made her appearance, and rushed with a shriek to her German.

A perfect Bedlam followed. Elena Ivanovna kept shrieking out the same phrase, as though in a frenzy, "Flay him! flay him!" [...]. The proprietor and Mutter took no notice whatever of either of us; they were both bellowing like calves over the tank. [...]

"He did for himself! He will burst himself at once, for he did swallow a ganz official!" cried the proprietor.

"*Unser Karlchen, unser allerliebster Karlchen wird sterben,*" howled his wife.

"We are orphaned and without bread!" chimed in the proprietor.

"Flay him! flay him! flay him!" clamored Elena Ivanovna, clutching at the German's coat.

"He did tease the crocodile. For what did your husband tease the crocodile?" cried the German, pulling away from her. "You will pay, if Karlchen *wird burst, das war mein Sohn, das war mein einziger Sohn.*"

I must own I was intensely indignant at the sight of such egoism in the German and the cold-heartedness of his dishevelled Mutter; at the same time Elena Ivanovna's reiterated shriek of "Flay him! flay him!" trubled me even more and absorbed at last my whole attention, positively alarming me. [...] Looking round at the door, not without embarrassment, I began to entreat Elena Ivanovna to calm herself, and above all not to use the shocking word "flay." For such a reactionary desire here, in the midst of

Не могу́ да́же и поду́мать вы́разить, до како́й сте́пени было си́льно волне́ние Еле́ны Ива́новны в продолже́ние всего́ проце́сса. Снача́ла, после пе́рвого кри́ка, она́ как бы замерла́ на ме́сте и смотре́ла на представля́вшуюся ей кутерьму́, по-ви́димому, равноду́шно [...]; пото́м вдруг залила́сь раздира́ющим во́плем [...].

В э́то мгнове́ние и хозя́ин, снача́ла то́же отупе́вший от у́жаса, вдруг всплесну́л рука́ми и закрича́л, гля́дя на не́бо:

— О мой крокоди́ль, о мейн аллерли́бстер Ка́рльхен! Му́ттер, му́ттер, му́ттер!

На э́тот крик отвори́лась за́дняя дверь и показа́лась му́ттер, в чепце́, румя́ная, пожила́я, но растрёпанная, и с ви́згом бро́силась к своему́ не́мцу.

Тут-то начался́ содо́м: Еле́на Ива́новна выкри́кивала, как исступлённая, одно́ то́лько сло́во: «Вспоро́ть! вспоро́ть!» [...]. Хозя́ин же и му́ттер ни на кого́ из нас не обраща́ли внима́ния: они́ о́ба вы́ли, как теля́та, о́коло я́щика. [...]

— Он пропади́ль, он сейча́с бу́дет ло́паль, потому́ что он проглати́ль ганц чино́вник! — крича́л хозя́ин.

— Унзер Ка́рльхен, унзер аллерли́бстер Ка́рльхен вирд штербен! — вы́ла хозя́йка.

— Мы сиро́тт и без клеб! — подхва́тывал хозя́ин.

— Вспоро́ть, вспоро́ть, вспоро́ть! — залива́лась Еле́на Ива́новна, вцепи́вшись в сюрту́к не́мца.

— Он дразни́ль крокоди́ль, — заче́м ваш муж дразни́ль крокоди́иль! — крича́л, отбива́ясь, не́мец, — вы запла́тит, е́сли Ка́рльхен вирд ло́паль, — дас вар мейн зон, дас вар мейн а́йнцигер зон!

Признаю́сь, я был в стра́шном негодова́нии, ви́дя тако́й эгои́зм зае́зжего не́мца и су́хость се́рдца в его́ растрёпанной му́ттер; тем не ме́нее беспреры́вно повторя́емые кри́ки Еле́ны Ива́новны: «Вспоро́ть, вспоро́ть!» — ещё бо́лее возбужда́ли моё беспоко́йство и увлекли́ наконе́ц всё моё внима́ние, та́к что я да́же испуга́лся... [...] Не бе́з смуще́ния озира́ясь на дверь, на́чал я упра́шивать Еле́ну Ива́новну успоко́иться и, гла́вное, не употребля́ть щекотли́вого сло́ва «вспоро́ть», и́бо тако́е ретрогра́дное

the Passazh and of the most educated society, not two paces from the hall where at this very minute Mr. Lavrov was perhaps delivering a public lecture, was not only impossible but unthinkable […]. To my horror I was immediately proved to be correct in my alarmed suspicions: the curtain [...] suddenly parted, and in the opening there appeared a figure with moustaches and beard, carrying a cap [...].

"Such a reactionary desire, madam," said the stranger, [...] "does no credit to your development, and is conditioned by lack of phosphorus in your brain. You will be promptly held up to shame in the Chronicle of Progress and in our satirical prints ..."

But he could not complete his remarks; the proprietor coming to himself, and seeing with horror that a man was talking in the crocodile room without having paid entrance money, rushed furiously at the progressive stranger and turned him out with a punch from each fist. [...]

"You wish that my crocodile be perished!" the proprietor yelled, running in again. "No! let your husband be perished first, before my crocodile!... Mein Vater showed crocodile, mein Grossvater showed crocodile, mein Sohn will show crocodile, and I will show crocodile! [...] you must pay me a Strafe!" [...]

"And, indeed, it's useless to flay the creature," I added calmly, [...] "as our dear Ivan Matveich is by now probably soaring somewhere in the empyrean."

"My dear" – we suddenly heard, to our intense amazement, the voice of Ivan Matveich – "my dear, my advice is to apply direct to the superintendent's office, as without the assistance of the police the German will never be made to see reason."

These words, uttered with firmness and aplomb, and expressing an exceptional presence of mind, at first so astounded us that we could not believe our ears. [...] His voice was muffled, thin and even squeaky, as though it came from a considerable distance. [...]

"Ivan Matveich, my dear, so, you're alive!" faltered Elena Ivanovna.

жела́ние здесь, в са́мом се́рдце Пасса́жа и образо́ванного о́бщества, в двух шага́х от той са́мой за́лы, где, мо́жет быть, в э́ту са́мую мину́ту господи́н Лавро́в чита́л публи́чную ле́кцию, — не то́лько бы́ло невозмо́жно но да́же немы́слимо [...]. К у́жасу моему́, я неме́дленно оказа́лся прав в пугли́вых подозре́ниях мои́х: вдруг раздви́нулась за́навесь, [...] и на поро́ге показа́лась фигу́ра с уса́ми, с бородо́й и с фура́жкой в рука́х [...].

— Тако́е ретрогра́дное жела́ние, суда́рыня, — сказа́л незнако́мец, [...] — не де́лает че́сти ва́шему разви́тию и обусло́вливается недоста́тком фо́сфору в ва́ших мозга́х. Вы неме́дленно бу́дете освистаны в хро́нике прогре́сса и в сатири́ческих листка́х на́ших...

Но он не доко́нчил: опо́мнившийся хозя́ин, с у́жасом уви́дев челове́ка, говоря́щего в крокоди́льной и ничего́ за э́то не заплати́вшего, с я́ростию бро́сился на прогресси́вного незнако́мца и обо́ими кулака́ми вы́толкал его́ в ше́ю. [...]

— Ви хати́т, чтоб мой крокоди́ль пропади́ль! — завопи́л вбежа́вший опя́ть хозя́ин, — нетт, пуска́й ваш муж сперва́ пропади́ль, а потом крокоди́ль!.. Мейн фа́тер показа́ль крокоди́ль, мейн гросфа́тер показа́ль крокоди́ль, мейн зон бу́дет показа́ть крокоди́ль, и я бу́дет показа́ть крокоди́ль! [...] мне пла́тит штраф. [...]

— Да и бесполе́зно вспа́рывать, — споко́йно приба́вил я [...] — и́бо наш ми́лый Ива́н Матве́ич, по всей вероя́тности, пари́т, тепе́рь где-нибу́дь в эмпире́ях.

— Друг мой, — разда́лся в э́ту мину́ту соверше́нно, неожи́данно го́лос Ива́на Матве́ича, изуми́вший нас до кра́йности, — друг мой, моё мне́ние — де́йствовать пря́мо че́рез конто́ру надзира́теля, и́бо не́мец без по́мощи поли́ции не поймёт и́стины.

Э́ти слова́, вы́сказанные твёрдо, с ве́сом и выража́вшие прису́тствие ду́ха необыкнове́нное, снача́ла до того́ изуми́ли нас, что мы все отказа́лись бы́ло ве́рить уша́м на́шим. [...] Го́лос его́ был заглушённый, то́ненький и да́же крикли́вый, как бу́дто выходи́вший из значи́тельного от нас отдале́ния. [...]

— Ива́н Матве́ич, друг мой, ита́к, ты жив! — лепета́ла Еле́на Ива́новна.

"Alive and well," answered Ivan Matveich, "and, thanks to the Almighty, swallowed without any damage whatever. I'm only uneasy as to the view my superiors may take of the incident; for after getting a permit to go abroad I've got into a crocodile, which seems anything but clever."

"But, my dear, don't truble your head about being clever; first of all we must somehow excavate you from where you are," Elena Ivanovna interrupted.

"Excavate!" cried the proprietor. "I will not let my crocodile be excavated. Now the Publicum will come many more, and I will funfzig kopeks ask and Karlchen will cease to burst."

"*Gott sei Dank!*" put in his wife.

"They're right," Ivan Matveich observed tranquilly; "the economic principle before everything."

"My friend! I will fly at once to the authorities and lodge a complaint, for I feel that we cannot settle this mess by ourselves."

"I think so too." observed Ivan Matveich; "but in our age of industrial crisis it is not easy to rip open the belly of a crocodile without economic compensation, and meanwhile the inevitable question presents itself: what will the German take for his crocodile? And with it another: who will pay?" […]

"I will not the crocodile sell; I will for three thousand the crocodile sell! I will for four thousand the crocodile sell! Now the Publicum will come very many. I will for five thousand the crocodile sell!" […]

"You'd better go today to Timofey Semyonich, as though it's an ordinary visit; he is an old-fashioned and by no means brilliant man, but he is trustworthy, and what matters most of all, straightforward. […] And meanwhile take Elena Ivanovna home…. Calm yourself, my dear," he continued, addressing her. "I'm weary of these outcries and feminine squabblings, and should like a nap. It's soft and warm in here, though I have hardly had time to look round in this unexpected haven."

"Look round! Why, is it light in there?" cried Elena Ivanovna in a tone of relief.

— Жив и здоро́в, — отвеча́л Ива́н Матве́ич, — и благодаря́ всевы́шнего проглочен без вся́кого поврежде́ния. Беспоко́юсь же еди́нственно о том, как взгля́нет на сей эпизо́д нача́льство; и́бо, получи́в биле́т за грани́цу, угоди́л в крокоди́ла, что да́же и неостроу́мно...

— Но, друг мой, не забо́ться об остроу́мии; пре́жде всего́ на́добно тебя́ отсю́да ка́к-нибу́дь вы́ковырять, — прервала́ Еле́на Ива́новна.

— Ковыря́йт! — вскрича́л хозя́ин, — я не дам ковыря́йт крокоди́ль. Тепе́рь пу́бликум бу́дет о́шень бо́льше ходи́ль, а я бу́ду фу́фциг копе́ек проси́ль, и Ка́рльхен переста́нет ло́паль. [...]

— Они́ пра́вы, — споко́йно заме́тил Ива́н Матве́ич, — экономи́ческий при́нцип пре́жде всего́.

— Друг мой, — закрича́л я, — сейча́с же лечу́ по нача́льству и бу́ду жа́ловаться, и́бо предчу́вствую, что нам одни́м э́той ка́ши не свари́ть.

— И я то́же ду́маю, — заме́тил Ива́н Матве́ич, — но без экономи́ческого вознагражде́ния тру́дно в наш век торго́вого кри́зиса да́ром вспоро́ть брю́хо крокоди́лово, а ме́жду тем представля́ется неизбе́жный вопро́с: что возьмёт хозя́ин за своего́ крокоди́ла? а с ним и друго́й: кто запла́тит? [...]

— Я не продава́йт крокоди́ль, я три ты́сячи продава́йт крокоди́ль, я четы́ре ты́сячи продава́йт крокоди́ль! Тепе́рь пу́убликум бу́дет мно́го ходи́ль. Я пять ты́сяч продава́йт крокоди́ль! [...]

— А заезжа́й-ка ты лу́чше сего́дня, так, в ви́де ча́стного посеще́ния, к Тимофе́ю Семе́нычу. Челове́к он старомо́дный и недалёкий, но соли́дный и, гла́вное, — прямо́й. [...] А тепе́рь уведи́ пока́ Еле́ну Ива́новну... Успоко́йся, друг мой, — продолжа́л он ей, — я уста́л от всех э́тих кри́ков и ба́бьих дрязг и жела́ю немно́го соснӳ́ть. Здесь же тепло́ и мя́гко, хотя́ я и не успе́л ещё осмотре́ться в э́том неожи́данном для меня́ убе́жище...

— Осмотре́ться! Ра́зве тебе́ там светло́? — вскри́кнула обра́дованная Еле́на Ива́новна.

"I am surrounded by impenetrable night," answered the poor captive, "but I can feel and, so to speak, have a look round with my hands.... [...] Till tomorrow! And you, Semyon Semyonich, come to me in the evening [...]."

I confess I was glad to get away, for I was overtired and somewhat bored. Hastening to offer my arm to the disconsolate Elena Ivanovna, whose charms were only enhanced by her agitation, I hurriedly led her out of the crocodile room.

"The charge will be another quarter-ruble in the evening," the proprietor called after us.

"Oh, dear, how greedy they are!" said Elena Ivanovna, looking at herself in every mirror on the walls of the Passazh, and evidently aware that she was looking prettier than usual.

"The economic principle," I answered with some emotion [...].

"The economic principle," she drawled in a touching little voice. "I did not in the least understand what Ivan Matveich said about that horrid economic principle just now. [...] Poor Ivan Matveich," she added a minute later, putting her little head on one side coquettishly. "I am really sorry for him. Oh, dear!" she cried suddenly, "how is he going to have his dinner... and... and... what will he do... if he wants anything? [...] Poor dear! how could he have got into such a mess ... [...]. How vexing it is that I have no photograph of him. And so now I'm a sort of widow," she added, with a seductive smile, evidently interested in her new position. "Hm! ... I am sorry for him, though."

It was, in short, the expression of the very natural and intelligible grief of a young and interesting wife for the loss of her husband. I took her home at last, soothed her, and [...] set off at six o'clock to Timofey Semyonich [...].

— Меня́ окружа́ет непробу́дная ночь, — отвеча́л бе́дный у́зник, — но я могу́ щу́пать и, так сказа́ть, осма́триваться рука́ми... [...] До за́втра! Ты же, Семён Семе́ныч, побыва́й ко мне ве́чером. [...]

Признаю́сь, я и рад был уйти́, потому́ что сли́шком уста́л, да отча́сти и наску́чило. Взяв поспе́шно под ру́чку уны́лую, но похороше́вшую от волне́ния Еле́ну Ива́новну, я поскоре́е вы́вел её из крокоди́ильной.

— Ве́чером за вход опя́ть четверта́к! — кри́кнул нам вслед хозя́ин.

— О бо́же, как они́ жа́дны! — проговори́ла Еле́на Ива́новна, глядя́сь в ка́ждое зе́ркало в просте́нках Пасса́жа и, ви́димо, сознава́я, что она́ похороше́ла.

— Экономи́ческий при́нцип, — отвеча́л я с лёгким волне́нием [...].

— Экономи́ческий при́нцип... — протяну́ла она́ симпати́ческим голоско́м, — я ничего́ не поняла́, что говори́л сейча́с Ива́н Матве́ич об э́том проти́вном экономи́ческом при́нципе. [...] Бе́дный Ива́н Матве́ич, — приба́вила она́ че́рез мину́ту, коке́тливо склони́в на плечо́ голо́вку, — мне, пра́во, его́ жаль, ах бо́же мой! — вдруг вскри́кнула она́, — скажи́те, ка́к же он бу́дет сего́дня там ку́шать и... и... ка́к же он бу́дет... Е́сли ему́ чего́-нибу́дь бу́дет на́добно? [...] Бедня́жка, как э́то он так втю́рился... [...] как доса́дно, что у меня́ не оста́лось его́ фотографи́ческой ка́рточки... Ита́к, я тепе́рь вро́де вдовы́, — приба́вила она́ с обольсти́тельной улы́бкой, очеви́дно интересу́ясь но́вым свои́м положе́нием, — гм... всё-таки мне его́ жаль!..

Одни́м сло́вом, выража́лась весьма́ поня́тная и есте́ственная тоска́ молодо́й и интере́сной жены́ о поги́бшем му́же. Я привёл её наконе́ц домо́й, успоко́ил и [...] отпра́вился в шесть часо́в к Тимофе́ю Семе́нычу [...].

II

The venerable Timofey Semyonich met me rather nervously, as though somewhat embarrassed. [...]

"First of all," he said, "take note that I'm [...] just such a subordinate official as you and Ivan Matveich.... I have nothing to do with it, and do not intend to mix myself up in the affair."

I was surprised to find that he apparently knew all about it already. [...] He listened without special surprise, but with evident signs of suspicion.

"Only fancy," he said, "I always believed that this was sure to happen to him."

"Why, Timofey Semyonich? It's a very unusual incident in itself ..."

"I agree. But Ivan Matveich's whole career in the service was leading up to this end. He's flighty, conceited even. It was always "progress" and ideas of all sorts, and this is what progress leads to!"

"But this is a most unusual incident and can't possibly serve as a general rule for all progressives."

"Yes, indeed it can. You see, it's the effect of over-education, I assure you. For over-education leads people to poke their noses into all sorts of places, especially where they're not invited. Though perhaps you know best," he added, as though offended. [...]

"Oh, no, Timofey Semyonich, not at all. On the contrary, Ivan Matveich is eager for your advice; he's eager for your guidance. He implores it, so to say, with tears."

"So to say, with tears! Hm! Those are crocodile tears and one can't quite believe in them." [....]

"Oh, come, Timofey Semyonich! [...] Have pity at least on the unfortunate Elena Ivanovna!"

"You're speaking of his wife? A charming little lady," said Timofey Semyonich, visibly softening and taking a pinch of snuff with relish.

II

Почтённый Тимофей Семёныч встретил меня ка́к-то торопли́во и как бу́дто немно́го смеша́вшись. [...]

— Пре́жде всего́, — на́чал он, — возьми́те во внима́ние, что я [...] тако́й же то́чно поднача́льный челове́к, ка́к и вы, ка́к и Ива́н Матве́ич... Я сторона́-с и ввя́зываться ни во что не наме́рен.

Я удиви́лся, что, по-ви́димому, он уже всё э́то зна́ет. [...] Он вы́слушал без осо́бого удивле́ния, но с я́вным при́знаком подозри́тельности.

— Предста́вьте, — сказа́л он, вы́слушав, — я всегда́ полага́л, что с ним непреме́нно э́то случи́тся.

— Почему́ же-с, Тимофе́й Семёныч, слу́чай са́м по себе́ весьма́ необыкнове́нный-с...

— Согла́сен. Но Ива́н Матве́ич во всё тече́ние слу́жбы свое́й и́менно клони́л к тако́му результа́ту. Пры́ток-с, зано́счив да́же. Всё «прогре́сс» да ра́зные иде́и-с, а во́т куда́ прогре́сс-то приво́дит!

— Но ведь э́то слу́чай са́мый необыкнове́нный, и о́бщим пра́вилом для всех прогресси́стов его́ ника́к нельзя́ положи́ть...

— Нет, уж э́то так-с. Это, ви́дите ли, от изли́шней образо́ванности происхо́дит, пове́рьте мне-с, и́бо лю́ди изли́шне образо́ванные ле́зут во вся́кое ме́сто-с и преиму́щественно туда́, где их во́все не спра́шивают. Впро́чем, мо́жет, вы бо́льше зна́ете, — приба́вил он, как бы обижа́ясь. [...]

— О нет, Тимофе́й Семёныч, поми́луйте. Напро́тив, Ива́н Матве́ич жа́ждет ва́шего сове́та, руково́дства ва́шего жа́ждет. Да́же, так сказа́ть, со слеза́ми-с.

— «Так сказа́ть со слеза́ми-с». Гм. Ну, э́то слёзы крокоди́ловы, и им не совсе́м мо́жно ве́рить. [...]

— Тимофе́ей Семёныч, поми́луйте [...]. Пожале́йте хоть несча́стную Еле́ну Ива́новну!

— Э́то вы про супру́гу-с? Интере́сная да́мочка, — проговори́л Тимофе́й Семёныч, ви́димо смягча́ясь и с аппети́том нюхну́в табаку́. — Осо́ба

"Particularly prepossessing. And so plump, and always putting her pretty little head on one side. ... Very agreeable." [...]

Timofey Semyonich blew his nose with a loud noise. [...]

"Well, what do you say then, Timofey Semyonich?" [...]

"If you ask my advice, you had better, above all, hush the matter up and act, so to speak, as a private person. It's a suspicious incident, quite unheard of. Unheard of, above all; there is no precedent for it, and it's far from creditable... So discretion above all... [...] And as for the German, it's my personal opinion he is within his rights, [...] because it was the other party who got into his crocodile without permission [...]. And a crocodile is private property, and so it is impossible to slit him open without compensation. [...] the so-called economic principle applies to the matter. And the economic principle is paramount. Only the other evening, at Luke Andreich's, Ignaty Prokofych was saying so. [...] 'We need industrial development', he said; 'there's very little development here. We must create it. We must create capital, so we must create a middle-class, a so-called bourgeoisie. And as we haven't capital we must attract it from abroad. We must, in the first place, give facilities to foreign companies to buy up lands in Russia as is done now abroad. The communal holding of land is poison,' he said, 'it's ruin. [...] With the communal system', he said, 'there will be no improvement in industrial development or agriculture. Foreign companies,' he said, 'must as far as possible buy up the whole of our land in big lots, and then split it up, split it up, split it up, in the smallest parts possible [...] and then sell it as private property. [...] When', he said, 'all the land is in the hands of foreign companies they can fix any rent they like. And so the peasant will work three times as much for his daily bread and he can be turned out at will. So that he will feel it, will be submissive and industrious, and will work three times as much for the same wages. But as it is, with the commune, what does he care? He knows he won't die of hunger, so he's lazy and drunken. And meanwhile money will be attracted into Russia, capital will be created and the bourgeoisie will spring up.' Ignaty Prokofych speaks well. He's an orator. [...]"

субти́льная. И как полна́, и голо́вку всё так на бочо́к, на бочо́к... о́чень прия́тно-с. [...]

Тимофе́й Семёныч с тре́ском вы́сморкался. [...]

— Так ка́к же, Тимофе́й Семёныч?

— [...] е́сли хоти́те сове́та, то пре́жде всего́ на́до э́то де́ло замя́ть и де́йствовать, так сказа́ть, в ви́де ча́стного лица́. Слу́чай подозри́тельный-с, да́ и небыва́лый. Гла́вное, небыва́лый, приме́ра не́ было-с, да́ и пло́хо рекоменду́ющий... Поэ́тому осторо́жность пре́жде всего́... [...] А что́ каса́ется не́мца, то, по моему́ ли́чному мне́нию, он в своём пра́ве, [...] потому́ что в его́ крокоди́ла вле́зли без спро́су [...]. Ну-с, а крокоди́л составля́ет со́бственность, ста́ло быть, без вознагражде́ния его́ взре́зать нельзя́-с. [...] тут уже́ так называ́емый экономи́ческий при́нцип в де́йствии. А экономи́ческий при́нцип пре́жде всего́-с. Ещё тре́тьего дня у Луки́ Андре́ича на ве́чере Игна́тий Проко́фьич говори́л [...]: «Нам нужна́,» говори́т, «промы́шленность, промы́шленности у нас ма́ло. На́до её роди́ть. На́до капита́лы роди́ть, зна́чит, сре́днее сосло́вие, так называ́емую буржуази́ю на́до роди́ть. А та́к как нет у нас капита́лов, зна́чит, на́до их из-за грани́цы привле́чь. На́до, во-пе́рвых, дать ход иностра́нным компа́ниям для ску́пки по уча́сткам на́ших земе́ль, как везде́ утверждено́ тепе́рь за грани́цей. Общи́нная со́бственность — яд,» говори́т, «ги́бель! [...] С общи́ной, говори́т, ни промы́шленность, ни земледе́лие не возвы́сятся. На́до,» говори́т, «чтоб иностра́нные компа́нии скупи́ли по возмо́жности всю на́шу зе́млю по частя́м, а пото́м дроби́ть, дроби́ть, дроби́ть как мо́жно в ме́лкие уча́стки, [...] а пото́м и продава́ть в ли́чную со́бственность. [...] Когда́,» говори́т, «вся земля́ бу́дет у привлечённых иностра́нных компа́ний в рука́х, тогда́, зна́чит, мо́жно каку́ю уго́дно це́ну за аре́нду назна́чить. Ста́ло быть, мужи́к бу́дет рабо́тать уже́ втро́е, из одного́ насу́щного хле́ба, и его́ мо́жно когда́ уго́дно согна́ть. Зна́чит, он бу́дет чу́вствовать, бу́дет поко́рен, приле́жен и втро́е за ту же це́ну вы́работает. А тепе́рь в общи́не что ему́! Зна́ет, что с го́лоду не помрёт, ну́ и ле́нится, и пья́нствует. А меж те́м к нам и де́ньги привлеку́тся, и капита́лы заведу́тся, и буржуази́я пойдёт. [...]» Хорошо́ говори́т Игна́тий Проко́фьич. Ора́тор-с. [...]

"But how about Ivan Matveich?" I put in [...].

"How about Ivan Matveich? Why, I'm coming to that. Here we are, anxious to bring foreign capital into the country – and only consider: as soon as the capital of a foreigner, who has been attracted to Petersburg, has been doubled through Ivan Matveich, instead of protecting the foreign capitalist, we're proposing to rip open the belly of his original capital [...]. To my mind, Ivan Matveich, as the true son of his fatherland, ought to rejoice and to be proud that through him the value of a foreign crocodile has been doubled and possibly even trebled. That's just what is wanted to attract capital. If one man succeeds, mind you, another will come with a crocodile, and a third will bring two or three of them at once, and capital will grow up about them – there you have a bourgeoisie. It must be encouraged."

"For pity's sake, Timofey Semyonich!" I cried, "you're demanding almost supernatural self-sacrifice from poor Ivan Matveich."

"I demand nothing, and I beg you, before everything – as I have said already – to remember that I am not a person in authority and so can demand nothing of anyone. [....] What possessed him to get into the crocodile? A respectable man, a man of good grade in the service, lawfully married – and then to behave like that! Is it consistent?"

"But it was an accident."

"Who knows?"

[...] "The proprietor was at first alarmed that the crocodile would burst, but as soon as he was sure that it was all right, he began to bluster and was delighted to think that he could double the charge for entry."

"Treble and quadruple perhaps! The public will simply stampede the place now, and crocodile owners are smart people. [...] The important thing is that Ivan Matveich should remain anonymous, don't let him be in a hurry. Let everybody know, perhaps, that he's in the crocodile, but unofficially. Ivan Matveich is in particularly favorable circumstances for that, for he is reckoned to be abroad. It will be said he's in the crocodile, and we'll refuse to believe it. That's how it can be managed. The great thing is that he should wait; and why should he be in a hurry?" [...]

— Так ка́к же Ива́н-то Матве́ич? — вверну́л я [...].

— Ива́н-то Матве́ич как-с? Так ведь я к тому́ и клоню́-с. Са́ми же мы вот хлопо́чем о привлече́нии иностра́нных капита́лов в оте́чество, а во́т посуди́те: едва́ то́лько капита́л привлечённого крокоди́льщика удво́ился че́рез Ива́на Матве́ича, а мы, чём бы протежи́ровать иностра́нного со́бственника, напро́тив, стара́емся са́мому-то основно́му капита́лу брю́хо вспоро́ть. [...] По-мо́ему, Ива́н Матве́ич, как и́стинный сын оте́чества, до́лжен ещё ра́доваться и горди́ться тем, что собо́ю це́нность иностра́нного крокоди́ла удво́ил, а пожа́луй, ещё и утро́ил. Э́то для привлече́ния на́добно-с. Уда́стся одному́, смо́тришь, и друго́й с крокоди́лом прие́дет, а тре́тий уж двух и трёх зара́з привезёт, а о́коло них капита́лы группиру́ются. Вот и́ буржуази́я. На́добно поощря́ть-с.

— Поми́луйте, Тимофе́й Семе́ныч! — вскрича́л я, — да вы тре́буете почти́ неесте́ственного самоотверже́ния от бе́дного Ива́на Матве́ича!

— Ничего́ я не тре́бую-с и пре́жде всего́ прошу́ вас — как уже́ и пре́жде проси́л — сообрази́ть, что я не нача́льство и, ста́ло бы́ть, тре́бовать ни от кого́ и ничего́ не могу́. [...]. Опя́ть-таки кто ж веле́л ему́ влезть в крокоди́ла? Челове́к соли́дный, челове́к изве́стного чи́на, состоя́щий в зако́нном бра́ке, и вдруг — тако́й шаг! Сообра́зно ли э́то?

— Но ведь э́тот шаг случи́лся неча́янно-с.

— А кто его́ зна́ет?

— [...] Крокоди́льщик снача́ла испуга́лся, что ло́пнет крокоди́л, а пото́м, как убеди́лся, что всё благополу́чно, зава́жничал и обра́довался, что мо́жет це́ну удво́ить.

— Утро́ить, учетвери́ть ра́зве! Пу́блика тепе́рь прихлы́нет, а крокоди́льщики ло́вкий наро́д. [...] пре́жде всего́ пусть Ива́н Матве́ич наблюда́ет инко́гнито, пусть не торо́пится. Пусть все, пожа́луй, зна́ют, что он в крокоди́ле, но не зна́ют официа́льно. В э́том отноше́нии Ива́н Матве́ич нахо́дится да́же в осо́бенно благоприя́тных обстоя́тельствах, потому́ что чи́слится за грани́цей. Ска́жут, что в крокоди́ле, а мы и не пове́рим. Э́то мо́жно так подвести́. Гла́вное — пусть выжида́ет, да и куда́ ему́ спеши́ть? [...]

"Can't we arrange," I said, "that, if he is destined to remain in the entrails of the monster [...], he should send in a petition to be reckoned as still serving?" [...]

"On what grounds?"

"As sent on a special commission."

"What commission and where?"

"Why, into the entrails, the entrails of the crocodile.... So to speak, for exploration, for investigation of the facts on the spot. It would, of course, be a novelty, but it's progressive and at the same time would show zeal for enlightenment."

[...] "To send a special official," he said at last, "to the insides of a crocodile to conduct a special inquiry is, in my personal opinion, an absurdity. It's not in the regulations. And what sort of special inquiry could there be there?"

"The scientific study of nature on the spot, in the living subject. The natural sciences are all the fashion nowadays, botany... He could live there and report his observations... For instance, concerning digestion or simply habits. For the sake of accumulating facts."

"[...] Well, I'm no great authority on that subject, indeed I'm no philosopher at all. You say 'facts' – we are overwhelmed with facts as it is, and don't know what to do with them. [...] Moreover, you will admit he will report facts, so to speak, lying down. And, can one do one's official duties lying down? That would be another novelty and a dangerous one; and again, there's no precedent for it. [...]"

"But no live crocodiles have been brought over before now, Timofey Semyonich."

"Hm ... yes," he reflected again. "[...] but consider, that if with the arrival of living crocodiles government clerks begin to disappear, and then on the grounds that they're warm and comfortable there, expect to receive the official sanction for their position, and then take their ease there... you must admit it would be a bad example. [...]

"Intercede for him, Timofey Semyonich!"

— Нельзя́ ли устро́ить так-с, — сказа́л я, — что уж е́сли суждено́ ему́ остава́ться в не́драх чудо́вища [...], нельзя́ ли пода́ть ему́ проше́ние о том, что́бы чи́слиться на слу́жбе? [...]

— На како́м же основа́нии?

— В ви́де командиро́вки...

— Како́й и куда́?

— Да в не́дра же, крокоди́ловы не́дра... Так сказа́ть, для спра́вок, для изуче́ния фа́ктов на ме́сте. Коне́чно, э́то бу́дет но́во, но ведь э́то прогресси́вно и в то же вре́мя пока́жет забо́тливость о просвеще́нии-с...

[...] — Командирова́ть осо́бого чино́вника, — сказа́л он наконе́ц, — в не́дра крокоди́ла для осо́бых поруче́ний, по моему́ ли́чному мне́нию, — неле́по-с. По шта́ту не полага́ется. Да́ и каки́е мо́гут бы́ть туда́ поруче́ния?

— Да для есте́ственного, так сказа́ть, изуче́ния приро́ды на ме́сте, в живье́-с. Ны́нче всё пошли́ есте́ственные нау́ки-с, бота́ника... Он бы там жил и сообща́л-с... ну, там о пищеваре́нии и́ли про́сто о нра́вах. Для скопле́ния фа́ктов-с.

— [...] Ну, в э́том я не силён, да́ и не фило́соф. Вы говори́те: фа́кты, — мы и без того́ зава́лены фа́ктами и не зна́ем, что с ни́ми де́лать. [...] И к тому́ ж, согласи́тесь, он бу́дет сообща́ть фа́кты, так сказа́ть, лёжа на боку́. А ра́зве мо́жно служи́ть, лёжа на боку́? э́то уж опя́ть нововведе́ние, и прито́м опа́сное-с; и опя́ть-таки приме́ра тако́го не было.[...]

— Но ведь и крокоди́лов живы́х не привози́ли до сих пор, Тимофе́й Семе́ныч.

— Гм, да... — он опя́ть заду́мался. — [...] Но опя́ть возьми́те и то́, что е́сли с появле́нием живы́х крокоди́лов начну́т исчеза́ть служа́щие и пото́м, на основа́нии того́, что там тепло́ и мя́гко, бу́дут тре́бовать туда́ командиро́вок, а пото́м лежа́ть на боку́... согласи́тесь са́ми — дурно́й приме́р-с. [...]

— Пораде́йте, Тимофе́й Семе́ныч.

"I will do my best. [...] And his wife ... is she alone now? Is she depressed?"

"You should call on her, Timofey Semyonich."

"I will. I thought of doing so before; it's a good opportunity.... And what on earth possessed him to go and look at the crocodile. Though, indeed, I should like to see it myself." [...]

I flew at once, of course, to the Passazh to tell poor Ivan Matveich all the news. And, indeed, I was moved by curiosity to know how he was getting on in the crocodile and how it was possible to live in a crocodile. [...] At times it really seemed to me as though it were all an outlandish, monstrous dream, especially as an outlandish monster was the chief figure in it.

III

And yet it was not a dream, but actual, indubitable fact. Would I be telling the story if it were not?

But to continue...

It was late, about nine o'clock, when I reached the Passazh, and I had to go into the crocodile room by the back entrance, for the German had closed the shop earlier than usual that evening. Now in the seclusion of domesticity, he was walking about in a greasy old frock-coat, but he seemed three times as pleased as he had been in the morning. It was evident that he had no apprehensions now, and that the "publicum" had come "many more."[...] Although the shop was closed, he charged me a quarter-ruble. What unnecessary exactitude! [...]

"Are you alive, are you alive, my educated friend?" I cried, as I approached the crocodile, expecting my words to reach Ivan Matveich from a distance and to flatter his vanity.

"Alive and well," he answered, as though from a long way off or from under the bed, though I was standing close beside him. "Alive and well; but of that later.... How are things?" [...]

— Похлопочу́-с. [...]. Супру́га-то... одна́ тепе́рь? Скуча́ет?

— Вы бы навести́ли, Тимофе́й Семе́ныч.

— Навещу́-с, я ещё да́веча поду́мал, да́ и слу́чай удо́бный... И заче́м, заче́м э́то его́ дёргало смотре́ть крокоди́ла! А впро́чем, я бы и сам жела́л посмотре́ть. [...]

Разуме́ется, я тотча́с полете́л в Пасса́ж обо́ всем сообщи́ть бедня́жке Ива́ну Матве́ичу. Да́ и любопы́тство разбира́ло меня́: как он там устро́ился в крокоди́ле и как э́то мо́жно жить в крокоди́ле? [...] Поро́й мне, пра́во, каза́лось, что всё э́то како́й-то чудо́вищный сон, тем бо́лее что и де́ло-то шло о чудо́вище...

III

И, одна́ко ж, э́то был не сон, а настоя́щая, несомне́нная действи́тельность. Ина́че — стал ли бы я и расска́зывать!

Но продолжа́ю...

В Пасса́ж я попа́л уже по́здно, о́коло девяти́ часо́в, и в крокоди́льную принуждён был войти́ с за́днего хода, потому́ что не́мец за́пер магази́н на э́тот раз ра́нее обыкнове́нного. Он расха́живал по-дома́шнему в како́м-то заса́ленном ста́ром сюртучи́шке, но сам ещё втро́е дово́льнее, чем да́веча у́тром. Ви́дно бы́ло, что он уже́ ничего́ не бои́тся и что «пу́бликум мно́го ходи́ль». [...] Несмотря́ на то, что магази́н был уже за́перт, он всё-таки взял с меня́ четверта́к. И что́ за нену́жная аккура́тность! [...]

— Жи́в ли, жи́в ли образо́ванный друг мой! — гро́мко вскрича́л я, подходя́ к крокоди́лу и наде́ясь, что слова́ мои́ ещё и́здали дости́гнут Ива́на Матве́ича и польстя́т его́ самолю́бию.

— Жив и здоро́в, — отвеча́л он, как бу́дто и́здали или как бы из-под крова́ти, хотя́ я стоя́л по́дле него́, — жив и здоро́в, но об э́том по́сле... Как дела́? [...]

I described to him my whole conversation with Timofey Semyonich down to the smallest detail. As I told my story I tried to express a resentful tone.

"The old man is right," Ivan Matveich pronounced. [...] "I am ready to admit, however, that your idea about a special commission is not altogether absurd. I certainly have a great deal to report, both from a scientific and from an ethical point of view. But now all this has taken a new and unexpected aspect, and it's not worthwhile to truble about mere salary. [...] Listen," he began dictatorially. "The public came today in masses. There was no room left in the evening, and the police came in to keep order. At eight o'clock, that is, earlier than usual, the proprietor thought it necessary to close the shop and end the exhibition to count the money he had taken and prepare for tomorrow more conveniently. So I know we can expect a whole fairground tomorrow. So we may assume that all the most cultivated people in the capital, the ladies of the best society, the foreign ambassadors, the leading lawyers and so on, will all be present. What's more, people will be flowing here from the remotest provinces of our vast and interesting empire. The upshot of it is that I'm in full public view, and though hidden to sight, I am preeminent. [...] Taught by experience, I shall be an example of greatness and resignation to fate! I shall be, so to say, a lectern from which to instruct mankind. The mere biological details I can furnish about the monster I am inhabiting are of priceless value. And so, far from grumbling at what has happened, I confidently hope for the most brilliant of careers."

"You won't find it wearisome?" I asked sarcastically. [...] "What on earth, what can this frivolous blockhead find to be so cocky about?" I muttered to myself. "He ought to be crying instead of being cocky."

"No!" he answered my observation sharply, "for I am full of great ideas, only now can I at leisure ponder over the amelioration of the lot of humanity. Truth and light will come forth now from the crocodile. I shall certainly develop a new theory of economic relations and I shall be proud of it [...]. I shall refute everything and be a new Fourier. [...] But to business. My wife?"

Я рассказа́л всю мою бесе́ду с Тимофе́ем Семе́нычем до после́дней подро́бности. Расска́зывая, я стара́лся вы́казать не́сколько оби́женный тон.

— Стари́к прав, — реши́л Ива́н Матве́ич [...]. — Гото́в, одна́ко, созна́ться, что и твоя́ иде́я насчёт командиро́вки не соверше́нно неле́па. Действи́тельно, мно́гое могу́ сообщи́ть и в нау́чном, и в нра́вственном отноше́нии. Но тепе́рь э́то всё принима́ет но́вый и неожи́данный вид и не сто́ит хлопота́ть из одного́ то́лько жа́лованья. [...] Слу́шай, — на́чал он повели́тельно, — пу́блики сего́дня приходи́ло це́лая бе́здна. К ве́черу не хвати́ло ме́ста, и для поря́дка яви́лась поли́ция. В во́семь часо́в, то́ есть ра́нее обыкнове́нного, хозя́ин нашёл да́же ну́жным запере́ть магази́н и прекрати́ть представле́ние, чтоб сосчита́ть привлечённые де́ньги и удо́бнее пригото́виться к за́втраму. Зна́ю, что за́втра соберётся це́лая я́рмарка. Таки́м о́бразом, на́до полага́ть, что все образо́ваннейшие лю́ди столи́цы, да́мы вы́сшего о́бщества, иноэ́мные посла́нники, юри́сты и про́чие здесь перебыва́ют. Ма́ло того́: ста́нут наезжа́ть из многосторо́нних прови́нций на́шей обши́рной и любопы́тной импе́рии. В результа́те — я у всех на виду́, и хоть спря́танный, но пе́рвенствую. [...] Нау́ченный о́пытом, предста́влю из себя́ приме́р вели́чия и смире́ния пе́ред судьбо́ю! Бу́ду, так сказа́ть, ка́федрой, с кото́рой начну́ поуча́ть челове́чество. Да́же одни́ есте́ственнонау́чные све́дения, кото́рые могу́ сообщи́ть об обита́емом мно́ю чудо́вище, — драгоце́нны. И потому́ не то́лько не ропщу́ на да́вешний слу́чай, но твёрдо наде́юсь на блиста́тельнейшую из карье́р.

— Не наску́чило бы? — заме́тил я ядови́то. [...] «С чего́, с чего́ э́та легкомы́сленная башка́ кура́жится! — скрежета́л я шёпотом про себя́. — Тут на́до пла́кать, а не кура́житься».

— Нет! — отвеча́л он ре́зко на моё замеча́ние, — и́бо весь прони́кнут вели́кими иде́ями, то́лько тепе́рь могу́ на досу́ге мечта́ть об улучше́нии судьбы́ всего́ челове́чества. Из крокоди́ла вы́йдет тепе́рь пра́вда и свет. Несомне́нно изобрету́ но́вую со́бственную тео́рию но́вых экономи́ческих отноше́ний и бу́ду горди́ться е́ю [...].. Опрове́ргну всё и бу́ду но́вый Фурье́. [...] Но к де́лу. Жена́?

[...] Meekly, though gnashing my teeth, I told him how I had left Elena Ivanovna. He did not even hear me out.

"I have special plans in regard to her," he began impatiently. "If I am celebrated here, I wish her to be celebrated there. Savants, poets, philosophers, foreign mineralogists, statesmen, after conversing in the morning with me, will visit her salon in the evening. [...] Every word of mine will be listened to, every utterance will be thought over, repeated, printed. [...] They shall understand at last what abilities they have allowed to vanish in the entrails of a monster. [...] To be ready for anything, Elena Ivanovna should buy an encyclopedia tomorrow [...], so that she may be able to converse on any topic. Above all, she should be sure to read the political leader in the *St. Petersburg News*, comparing it every day with the *Hairald*. I imagine that the proprietor will consent to take me sometimes with the crocodile to my wife's brilliant salon. I shall be in a tank in the middle of the magnificent drawing-room, and I'll scintillate with witticisms which I'll prepare in the morning. To the statesman I will impart my projects; to the poet I will speak in rhyme; with the ladies I can be amusing and charming without impropriety, since I shall be no danger to their husbands. To all the rest I shall serve as a pattern of resignation to fate and the will of Providence. I shall make my wife a brilliant literary lady; I shall bring her forward and explain her to the public; as my wife, she must be full of the most striking virtues [...]."

[...] "My friend," I asked him, "are you hoping for a long life? Tell me, in fact, are you well? How do you eat, how do you sleep, how do you breathe? I am your friend, and you must admit that the incident is most unnatural, and consequently my curiosity is most natural."

"Idle curiosity and nothing else," he pronounced sententiously, "but you shall be satisfied. You ask how I'm managing in the entrails of the monster? To begin with, the crocodile, to my astonishment, turns out to be perfectly empty. His inside consists of a sort of huge empty sack made of india rubber, like the rubber goods sold in Gorokhovaya Street, in Morskaya, and,

[...] Смире́нно, но опя́ть-таки скрежеща́ зуба́ми, рассказа́л я, как оста́вил Еле́ну Ива́новну. Он да́же и не дослу́шал.

— Име́ю на неё осо́бые ви́ды, — на́чал он нетерпели́во, — е́сли бу́ду знамени́т здесь, то хочу́, чтоб она́ была́ знамени́та там. Учёные, поэ́ты, фило́софы, зае́зжие минерало́ги, госуда́рственные мужи́ по́сле у́тренней бесе́ды со мной бу́дут посеща́ть по вечера́м её сало́н. [...] Ка́ждое сло́во моё бу́дет выслу́шиваться, ка́ждое изрече́ние обду́мываться, передава́ться, печа́таться. [...] Пойму́т наконе́ц, каки́м спосо́бностям да́ли исче́знуть в не́драх чудо́вища. [...] На вся́кий слу́чай пусть Еле́на Ива́новна за́втра же ку́пит энциклопеди́ческий слова́рь, [...] чтоб уме́ть говори́ть обо́ всех предме́тах. Ча́ще же всего́ пусть чита́ет premier-поли́тик «С. — Петербу́ргских изве́стий», сверя́я каждодне́вно с «Во́лосом.» Полага́ю, что хозя́ин согласи́тся иногда́ приноси́ть и меня́, вме́сте с крокоди́лом, в блестя́щий сало́н жены́ мое́й. Я бу́ду стоя́ть в я́щике среди́ великоле́пной гости́ной и бу́ду сы́пать остро́тами, кото́рые подберу́ ещё с утра́. Госуда́рственному му́жу сообщу́ мои́ прое́кты; с поэ́том бу́ду говори́ть в ри́фму; с да́мами бу́ду заба́вен и нра́вственно-мил, — та́к как вполне́ безопа́сен для их супру́гов. Всем остальны́м бу́ду служи́ть приме́ром поко́рности судьбе́ и во́ле провиде́ния. Жену́ сде́лаю блестя́щею литерату́рною да́мою; я её вы́двину вперёд и объясню́ её пу́блике; как жена́ моя́, она́ должна́ быть полна́ велича́йших досто́инств [...].

— Друг мой, — спроси́л я его́, — наде́ешься ли ты на долгове́чность? И вообще́ скажи́: здоро́в ли ты? Как ты ешь, как ты спишь, как ты ды́шишь? Я друг тебе́, и согласи́сь, что слу́чай сли́шком сверхъесте́ственный, а сле́довательно, любопы́тство моё сли́шком есте́ственно.

— Пра́здное любопы́тство и бо́льше ничего́, — отвеча́л он сентенцио́зно, — но ты бу́дешь удовлетворён. [...] Во-пе́рвых, крокоди́л, к удивле́нию моему́, оказа́лся соверше́нно пусто́й. Вну́тренность его́ состои́т как бы из огро́много пусто́го мешка́, сде́ланного из рези́нки, вро́де тех рези́новых изде́лий, кото́рые распространены́ у нас в Горо́ховой, в Морско́й и, е́сли

if I am not mistaken, in Voznesensky Prospect. Otherwise, if you think of it, how could I find room?"

"Is it possible?" I cried, in a surprise that may well be understood. "Can the crocodile be perfectly empty?"

"Perfectly," Ivan Matveich maintained sternly and impressively. "And in all probability, it is thus constructed by the laws of Nature. The crocodile possesses nothing but jaws furnished with sharp teeth, and besides the jaws, a tail of considerable length – that's all, properly speaking. The middle part between these two extremities is an empty space enclosed by something of the nature of natural rubber, probably really rubber."

"But the ribs, the stomach, the intestines, the liver, the heart?" I interrupted quite angrily.

"There is nothing, absolutely nothing of all that, and probably there never has been. [...] He's incredibly elastic. Indeed, you might, as the friend of the family, get in with me if you were generous and self-sacrificing enough – and even with you here there would be room to spare. I even think that in the last resort I might send for Elena Ivanovna. However, this void, hollow formation of the crocodile is quite in keeping with the teachings of natural science. [...] What is the fundamental characteristic of the crocodile? The answer is clear: to swallow human beings. How is one, in constructing the crocodile, to secure that he should swallow people? The answer is clearer still: construct him hollow. It was settled by physics long ago that Nature abhors a vacuum. Hence the inside of the crocodile must be hollow so that it may abhor the vacuum, and consequently swallow and so fill itself with anything it can come across. And that is the sole rational cause why every crocodile swallows men. [...] Even etymology supports me, for the very word crocodile means voracity. Crocodile – *crocodillo* – is evidently an Italian word, dating perhaps from the Egyptian Pharaohs, and evidently derived from the French verb *croquer*, which means to eat, to devour, in general to absorb nourishment. [...]"

не ошиба́юсь, на Вознесе́нском проспе́кте. Ина́че, сообрази́, мог ли бы я в нем помести́ться?

— Возмо́жно ли? — вскрича́л я в поня́тном изумле́нии. — Неуже́ли крокоди́л соверше́нно пусто́й?

— Соверше́нно, — стро́го и внуши́тельно подтверди́л Ива́н Матве́ич. — И, по всей вероя́тности, он устро́ен так по зако́нам само́й приро́ды. Крокоди́л облада́ет то́лько па́стью, снабжённою о́стрыми зуба́ми, и вдоба́вок к па́сти — значи́тельно дли́нным хвосто́м — вот и всё, по-настоя́щему. В середи́не же ме́жду си́ми двумя́ его́ оконе́чностями нахо́дится пусто́е простра́нство, обнесённое чем-то вро́де каучу́ка, вероя́тнее же всего́ действи́тельно каучу́ком.

— А рёбра, а желу́док, а кишки́, а пе́чень, а се́рдце? — прерва́л я да́же со зло́бою.

— Н-ничего́, соверше́нно ничего́ э́того нет и, вероя́тно, никогда́ не быва́ло. [...] Он растяжи́м до невероя́тности. Да́же ты, в ка́честве дома́шнего дру́га, мог бы помести́ться со мной ря́дом, е́сли б облада́л великоду́шием, — и да́же с тобо́й ещё доста́ло бы места. Я да́же ду́маю в кра́йнем слу́чае вы́писать сюда́ Еле́ну Ива́новну. Впро́чем, подо́бное пустопоро́жнее устро́йство крокоди́ла соверше́нно согла́сно с есте́ственными нау́ками. [...] како́е основно́е сво́йство крокоди́лово? Отве́т я́сен: глота́ть люде́й. Ка́к же дости́гнуть устро́йством крокоди́ла, чтоб он глота́л люде́й? Отве́т ещё ясне́е: устро́ив его́ пусты́м. Давно́ уже́ решено́ фи́зикой, что приро́да не те́рпит пустоты́. Подо́бно сему́ и вну́тренность крокоди́лова должна́ и́менно быть пусто́ю, чтоб не терпе́ть пустоты́, а, сле́дственно, беспреры́вно глота́ть и наполня́ться всем, что то́лько есть под руко́ю. И вот еди́нственная разу́мная причи́на, почему́ все крокоди́лы глота́ют на́шего бра́та. [...] Да́же этимоло́гия согла́сна со мно́ю, и́бо са́мое назва́ние крокоди́л означа́ет прожо́рливость. Крокоди́л, Crocodillo, — есть сло́во, очеви́дно, италья́нское, совреме́нное, мо́жет быть, дре́вним фарао́нам еги́петским и, очеви́дно, происходя́щее от францу́зского ко́рня: croquer, что означа́ет съесть, ску́шать и вообще́ употреби́ть в пи́щу. [...]

"But, my friend, how... how do you take food now? Have you dined today?"

"No, but I'm not hungry, and most likely I shall never take food again. And that, too, is quite natural; filling the whole interior of the crocodile I make him feel always full. Now he need not be fed for some years. On the other hand, nourished by me, he will naturally impart to me all the vital juices of his body [...]. In that way nourishing the crocodile, I myself obtain nourishment from him, consequently we mutually nourish one another. But as it's difficult even for a crocodile to digest a man like me, he must, no doubt, be conscious of a certain weight in his stomach – an organ which he does not, however, possess – and that's why, to avoid causing the creature suffering, I seldom turn over, and although I could turn over I do not do so from humanitarian motives. This is the one drawback of my present position, and in an allegorical sense Timofey Semyonich was right in saying I'm loafing about. But I will prove that even lying down – nay, only lying down – one can revolutionize the lot of mankind. [...] I am constructing now a complete system of my own, and you wouldn't believe how easy it is! You only have to creep into a secluded corner or into a crocodile and shut your eyes, and you immediately devise a complete paradise for all mankind. [...] it all becomes clearer, seen from the inside of the crocodile... There are some drawbacks, though small ones, in my position, however; it is somewhat damp here and covered with a sort of slime; and there is rather a smell of india-rubber, exactly like my old galoshes. That's all, there are no other drawbacks."

"Ivan Matveich," I interrupted, "all this is a miracle I can scarcely believe. And can you, can you intend never to dine again?"

"What trivial nonsense you are troubling about, you thoughtless, frivolous creature! I talk to you about great ideas, and you... Understand that I am sufficiently nourished by the great ideas that light up the darkness in which I am enveloped. [...] I hope to live at least a thousand

— Друг мой, а как... ка́к же ты тепе́рь употребля́ешь пи́щу? Обе́дал ты сего́дня и́ли нет?

— Нет, но сыт и, вероя́тнее всего́, тепе́рь уже́ никогда́ не бу́ду употребля́ть пи́щи. И э́то то́же соверше́нно поня́тно: наполня́я собо́ю всю вну́тренность крокоди́лову, я де́лаю его́ навсегда́ сы́тым. Тепе́рь его́ мо́жно не корми́ть не́сколько лет. С друго́й стороны́, — сы́тый мно́ю, он есте́ственно сообщи́т и мне все жи́зненные со́ки из своего́ те́ла [...]. Таки́м о́бразом, пита́я собо́ю крокоди́ла, я, обра́тно, получа́ю и от него́ пита́ние; сле́довательно — мы взаи́мно ко́рмим друг дру́га. Но та́к как тру́дно, да́же и крокоди́лу, перева́ривать тако́го челове́ка, как я, то уж, разуме́ется, он до́лжен при э́том ощуща́ть не́которую тя́жесть в желу́дке, — кото́рого, впро́чем, у него́ нет, — и во́т почему́, чтоб не доста́вить изли́шней бо́ли чудо́вищу, я ре́дко воро́чаюсь с бо́ку на́ бок; и хотя́ бы и мо́г воро́чаться, но не де́лаю сего́ из гума́нности. Это еди́нственный недоста́ток тепе́решнего моего́ положе́ния, и в аллегори́ческом смы́сле Тимофе́й Семе́ныч справедли́в, называ́я меня́ лежебо́кой. Но я докажу́, что и лёжа на боку́, — ма́ло того́, — что то́лько лёжа на боку́ и мо́жно переверну́ть судьбу́ челове́чества. [...] Я изобрету́ тепе́рь це́лую социа́льную систе́му, и — ты не пове́ришь — как э́то легко́! Сто́ит то́лько уедини́ться куда́-нибу́дь пода́льше в у́гол и́ли хо́ть попа́сть в крокоди́ла, закры́ть глаза́, и тотча́с же изобретёшь це́лый ра́й для всего́ челове́чества. [...] из крокоди́ла как бу́дто всё э́то видне́е стано́вится... Впро́чем, в моем положе́нии существу́ют и ещё недоста́тки, хотя́ и ме́лкие: внутри́ крокоди́ла не́сколько сы́ро и как бу́дто покры́то сли́зью да, сверх того́, ещё не́сколько па́хнет рези́нкой, точь-в-то́чь как от мои́х прошлого́дних кало́ш. Вот и́ всё, бо́лее нет никаки́х недоста́тков.

— Ива́н Матве́ич, — прерва́л я, — всё э́то чудеса́, кото́рым я едва́ могу́ ве́рить. И неуже́ли, неуже́ли ты всю жи́знь не наме́рен обе́дать?

— О како́м вздо́ре забо́тишься ты, беспе́чная, пра́здная голова́! Я тебе́ о вели́ких иде́ях расска́зываю, а ты... Знай же, что я сыт уже́ одни́ми вели́кими иде́ями, озари́вшими но́чь, меня́ окружи́вшую. [...]

years, if it is true that crocodiles live so long, which, by the way – good thing I thought of it – you'd better look up in some natural history tomorrow and tell me, for I may have been mistaken and have mixed it up with some other excavated monster. There's only one reflection rather troubling me: as I'm dressed in cloth and have boots on, the crocodile obviously can't digest me. Besides, I'm alive, and so am opposing the process of digestion with my whole will power; for you can understand that I do not wish to be turned into what all nourishment turns into, for that would be too humiliating for me. But there's one thing I'm afraid of: in a thousand years the cloth of my coat, unfortunately of Russian make, may decay, and then, left without clothing, I might perhaps, in spite of my indignation, begin to be digested; and though by day nothing would induce me to allow it, at night, in my sleep, when a man's will deserts him, I may be overtaken by the humiliating destiny of a potato, a pancake, or veal. Such an idea reduces me to fury. This alone is an argument for the revision of the tariff and the encouragement of the importation of English cloth, which is stronger and so will withstand Nature longer when one is swallowed by a crocodile. At the first opportunity I will impart this idea to some statesman and at the same time to the political writers on our Petersburg dailies." [...]

"My friend, and freedom?" I asked, wishing to learn his views thoroughly. "You are, so to speak, in prison, while every man has a right to the enjoyment of freedom."

"You're a fool. [...] Never has my spirit soared as now. [...] If not Socrates, then Diogenes, or perhaps both of them together – that is my future role among mankind." [...]

All that he told me about the crocodile struck me as most suspicious. How was it possible that the crocodile was absolutely hollow? I don't mind betting that he was bragging from vanity and partly to humiliate me. It's true that he was an invalid and one must make allowances for invalids; but I must frankly confess, I never could endure Ivan Matveich. [...]

Прожи́ть же наде́юсь по кра́йней ме́ре ты́сячу лет, е́сли справедли́во, что по сто́льку лет живу́т крокоди́лы, о чём, бла́го напо́мнил, спра́вься за́втра же в како́й-нибу́дь есте́ственной исто́рии и сообщи́ мне, и́бо я мог ошиби́ться, смеша́в крокоди́ла с каки́м-нибу́дь други́м ископа́емым. Одно́ то́лько соображе́ние не́сколько смуща́ет меня́: так как я оде́т в сукно́, а на нога́х у меня́ сапоги́, то крокоди́л, очеви́дно, меня́ не мо́жет перевари́ть. Сверх того́, я живо́й и потому́ сопротивля́юсь перева́рению меня́ все́ю мое́ю во́лею, и́бо поня́тно, что не хочу́ обрати́ться в то, во что обраща́ется вся́кая пи́ща, та́к как э́то бы́ло бы сли́шком для меня́ унизи́тельно. Но бою́сь одного́: в тысячеле́тний срок сукно́ сюртука́ моего́, к несча́стью ру́сского изде́лия, мо́жет истле́ть, и тогда́ я, оста́вшись без оде́жды, несмотря́ на всё моё негодова́ние, начну́, пожа́луй, и перева́риваться; и хоть днем я э́того ни за что́ не допущу́ и не позво́лю, но по ноча́м, во сне, когда́ во́ля отлета́ет от челове́ка, меня́ мо́жет пости́чь са́мая унизи́тельная у́часть како́го-нибу́дь карто́феля, блино́в и́ли теля́тины. Така́я иде́я приво́дит меня́ в бе́шенство. Уже́ по одно́й э́той причи́не на́до бы измени́ть тари́ф и поощря́ть приво́з су́кон англи́йских, кото́рые кре́пче, а сле́дственно, и до́льше бу́дут сопротивля́ться приро́де, в слу́чае е́сли попадёшь в крокоди́ла. При пе́рвом слу́чае сообщу́ мысль мою́ кому́-ли́бо из люде́й госуда́рственных, а вме́сте с тем и полити́ческим обозрева́телям на́ших ежедне́вных петербу́ргских газе́т. [...]

— Друг мой, а свобо́да? — проговори́л я, жела́я вполне́ узна́ть его́ мне́ние. — Ведь ты, так сказа́ть, в темни́це, тогда́ как челове́к до́лжен наслажда́ться свобо́дою.

— Ты глуп [...]. Никогда́ не воспаря́л я ду́хом так, как тепе́рь. [...] е́сли не Сокра́т, то Диоге́н, и́ли то и друго́е вме́сте, и во́т бу́дущая роль моя́ в челове́честве. [...]

Да и всё то, что сообщи́л он мне о крокоди́ле, показа́лось мне весьма́ подозри́тельным. Ну ка́к мо́жно, чтоб крокоди́л был соверше́нно пусто́й? Бью́сь об закла́д, что в э́том он прихвастну́л из тщесла́вия и отча́сти, чтоб меня́ уни́зить. Пра́вда, он был больно́й, а больно́му на́до ува́жить; но, признаю́сь открове́нно, я всегда́ терпе́ть не мог Ива́на Матве́ича. [...]

I can positively assert that nine-tenths of my friendship for him was made up of malice. On this occasion, however, we parted with genuine feeling.

"Your friend a very clever man is!" the German said to me in an undertone as he moved to see me out; he had been listening all the time attentively to our conversation.

"Apropos," I said, "while I think of it: how much would you ask for your crocodile in case anyone wanted to buy it?"

Ivan Matveich, who heard the question, was waiting with curiosity for the answer; it was evident that he did not want the German to ask too little [...].

At first the German would not listen – and was positively angry.

[…] "Me not want sell the crocodile! I will not for the crocodile a million thalers take. I took a hundred and thirty thalers from the public to-day, and I shall tomorrow ten thousand take, and then a hundred thousand every day I shall take. I will not him sell."

Ivan Matveich even chuckled with satisfaction.

Controlling myself – for I felt it was a duty to my friend – I hinted coolly and reasonably to the crazy German that his calculations were not quite correct, that if he were to make a hundred thousand every day, all Petersburg would have visited him in four days, and then there would be no one left to bring him rubles, that life and death are in God's hands, that the crocodile might burst somehow, or Ivan Matveich might fall ill and die, and so on and so on.

[…] "Consider, too, that the thing may get into the law courts. Ivan Matveich's wife may demand the restitution of her lawful spouse. You're intending to get rich, but do you intend to give Elena Ivanovna a pension?"

"No, me not intend," said the German in stern decision.

"No, he not intend," said the Mutter, with positive malignancy.

"And so would it not be better for you to accept something now, at once, a secure and solid though moderate sum, than to leave things to chance? [...]"

Положительно могу́ сказа́ть, что я на де́вять деся́тых был с ним дру́жен из зло́бы. На э́тот раз мы прости́лись, одна́ко же, с чу́вством.

— Ваш друк о́шень у́мна шелове́к, — сказа́л мне вполго́лоса не́мец, собира́ясь меня́ провожа́ть [...].

— А propos, — сказа́л я, — чтоб не забы́ть, — ско́лько бы взя́ли вы за ва́шего крокоди́ла, на слу́чай е́сли б взду́мали у вас его́ покупа́ть?

Ива́н Матве́ич, слы́шавший вопро́с, с любопы́тством выжида́л отве́та. Ви́димо бы́ло, что ему́ не хоте́лось, чтоб не́мец взял ма́ло [...].

Снача́ла не́мец и слу́шать не хоте́л, да́же рассерди́лся.

— [...] Я не хати́т продава́йт крокоди́ль. Я миллио́н та́лер не ста́ну браль за крокоди́ль. Я сто три́дцать та́лер сего́дня с пу́бликум браль, а за́втра де́сять ты́сяч та́лер собра́ль, а пото́м сто ты́сяч та́лер ка́ждый день собира́ль. Не хочу́ продава́ль!

Ива́н Матве́ич да́же захихи́кал от удово́льствия.

Скрепя́ се́рдце, хладнокро́вно и рассуди́тельно, — и́бо исполня́л обя́занность и́стинного дру́га, — намекну́л я сумасбро́дному не́мцу, что расчёты его́ не совсе́м ве́рны, что́ е́сли он ка́ждый день бу́дет собира́ть по сту ты́сяч, то в четы́ре дня у него́ перебыва́ет весь Петербу́рг и пото́м уже́ не́ с кого бу́дет собира́ть, что в животе́ и сме́рти во́лен бог, что крокоди́л мо́жет ка́к-нибу́дь ло́пнуть, а Ива́н Матве́ич заболе́ть и помере́ть и проч., и проч.

[...] — Возьми́те и то́, что мо́жет затея́ться суде́бный проце́сс. Супру́га Ива́на Матве́ича мо́жет потре́бовать своего́ зако́нного супру́га. Вы вот наме́рены богате́ть, а наме́рены ли вы назна́чить хоть каку́ю-нибу́дь пе́нсию Еле́не Ива́новне?

— Нет, не ме́реваль! — реши́тельно и стро́го отвеча́л не́мец.

— Нетт, не ме́реваль! — подхвати́ла, да́же со зло́бою, му́ттер.

— Ита́к, не лу́чше ли вам взять что-нибу́дь тепе́рь, ра́зом, хо́ть и уме́ренное, но ве́рное и соли́дное, чем предава́ться неизве́стности? [...]

After consultation with his Mutter he demanded for his crocodile fifty thousand rubles in bonds of the last Russian loan with a lottery ticket attached, a brick house in Gorokhovaya Street with its own chemist's shop, and in addition the rank of Russian colonel.

"You see!" Ivan Matveich cried triumphantly. "[...] he's perfectly right, for he fully understands the present value of the monster he's exhibiting. The economic principle before everything!"

"Upon my word!" I cried furiously to the German. "But what should you be made a colonel for? [...] In what way have you gained military glory? You are really insane!"

"Insane!" cried the German, offended. "[...] I have a colonel deserved for that I have a crocodile shown and in him a live Hofrath sitting! And a Russian can a crocodile not show and a live Hofrath in him sitting! Me extremely clever man and much wish to colonel be!"

"Well, good-bye, then, Ivan Matveich!" I cried, shaking with fury, and I went out of the crocodile room almost at a run. I felt that in another minute I could not have answered for myself. The unnatural expectations of these two blockheads were unbearable. The cold air refreshed me and somewhat moderated my indignation. At last, after spitting vigorously fifteen times on each side, I took a cab, got home, undressed and flung myself into bed. [...] All night long I dreamt of nothing but monkeys, but towards morning I dreamt of Elena Ivanovna.

IV

[...] Going over all the incidents of the previous day as I drank my morning cup of tea, I resolved to go and see Elena Ivanovna at once on my way to the office – which, indeed, I was bound to do as the friend of the family.

In a tiny little room by the bedroom, [...] in some half-transparent morning wrapper, on a smart little sofa before a little tea-table, Elena Ivanovna sat drinking coffee out of a little cup in which she was dipping

Насове́товавшись с свое́й му́ттер, он потре́бовал за своего́ крокоди́ла пятьдеся́т ты́сяч рубле́й биле́тами после́днего вну́треннего за́йма с лотере́ю, ка́менный дом в Горо́ховой и при нем со́бственную апте́ку и, вдоба́вок, — чин ру́сского полко́вника.

— Ви́дишь! — торжеству́я, прокрича́л Ива́н Матве́ич, — [...] он соверше́нно прав, и́бо вполне́ понима́ет тепе́решнюю це́нность пока́зываемого им чудо́вища. Экономи́ческий при́нцип пре́жде всего́!

— Поми́луйте! — я́ростно закрича́л я не́мцу, — да за что́ же вам полко́вника-то? [...] како́й вое́нной сла́вы доби́лись? Ну, не безу́мец ли вы по́сле э́того?

— Безу́мны! — вскрича́л не́мец оби́девшись, — [...] Я заслужи́ль полько́вник, потому́ што показа́ль крокоди́ль, а в нем живо́й гоф-рат сиди́ль, а ру́сский не мо́жет показа́ль крокоди́ль, а в нем живо́й гоф-рат сиди́ль! [...]

— Так проща́й же, Ива́н Матве́ич! — вскрича́л я, дрожа́ от бе́шенства, и почти́ бего́м вы́бежал из крокоди́льной. Я чу́вствовал, что ещё мину́та, и я уже́ не мо́г бы отвеча́ть за себя́. Неесте́ственные наде́жды э́тих двух болва́нов бы́ли невыноси́мы. Холо́дный во́здух, освежи́в меня́, не́сколько уме́рил моё негодова́ние. Наконе́ц, энерги́чески плю́нув раз до пятна́дцати в о́бе сто́роны, я взял изво́зчика, прие́хал домо́й, разде́лся и бро́сился в посте́ль. [...] Всю ночь сни́лись мне то́лько одни́ обезья́ны, но под са́мое у́тро присни́лась Еле́на Ива́новна...

IV

[...] перебира́я в голове́ за у́тренней ча́шкой ча́ю все происше́ствия вчера́шнего дня, я реши́л неме́дленно зайти́ к Еле́не Ива́новне, по доро́ге на слу́жбу, что, впро́чем, обя́зан был сде́лать и в ка́честве дома́шнего дру́га.

В кро́шечной ко́мнатке, пе́ред спа́льней, [...] на ма́леньком наря́дном дива́нчике, за ма́леньким ча́йным сто́ликом, в како́й-то полувозда́шной у́тренней распашо́ночке сиде́ла Еле́на Ива́новна и из ма́ленькой

a minute biscuit. She was ravishingly pretty, but struck me as being at the same time rather pensive.

"Ah, it's you, naughty man!" she said, greeting me with a distracted smile. […] Well, what were you doing yesterday?" […]

"Yesterday I was visiting our captive..." […]

"Whom?... What captive?... Oh, yes! Poor fellow! Well, how is he – bored? Do you know... I wanted to ask you... I suppose I can ask for a divorce now?"

"A divorce!" I cried in indignation and almost spilled the coffee. […]

"Why, […] if he is going to stay on in the crocodile, perhaps not come back all his life, while I sit waiting for him here! A husband ought to live at home, and not in a crocodile…."

"But this was an unforeseen occurrence," I was beginning, in very comprehensible agitation.

"Oh, no, don't talk to me, I won't listen, […]" she cried, suddenly getting quite cross. "[…] Other people tell me I can get a divorce because Ivan Matveich won't get his salary now."

"Elena Ivanovna! Is it you I hear!" I exclaimed pathetically. "[…] And divorce on such trivial grounds as salary is quite impossible. And poor Ivan Matveich […] is, so to speak, burning with love for you even in the bowels of the monster. […] Yesterday […] he was saying that he might as a last resort send for you as his lawful spouse to join him in the entrails of the monster, especially as it appears the crocodile is exceedingly roomy, able to accommodate not just two but even three persons..."

And then I told her all that interesting part of my conversation the night before with Ivan Matveich.

"What, what!" she cried, in surprise. "You want me to get into the monster too, to be with Ivan Matveich? What an idea! And how am I to get in there, in my hat and crinoline? Heavens, what idiocy! And what should I look like while I was getting into it, and very likely there would be someone there to see me! It's absurd! And what should I have to eat there? And... and... and what should I do there when... Oh, my goodness, what will they

чашечки, в которую макала крошечный сухарик, кушала кофе. Была она обольстительно хороша, но показалась мне тоже и как будто задумчивою.

— Ах, это вы, шалун! — встретила она меня с рассеянной улыбкой, — садитесь, ветреник, пейте кофе. Ну что вы вчера делали? [...]

— Посещал вчера нашего узника...

— Кого? Какого это узника? Ах, да! Бедняжка! Ну, что он — скучает? А знаете... я хотела вас спросить... Я ведь могу теперь просить развода?

— Развода! — вскричал я в негодовании и чуть не пролил кофе. [...]

— Да что ж, [...] что ж он там будет сидеть в крокодиле и, пожалуй, всю жизнь не придёт, а я здесь его дожидайся! Муж должен дома жить, а не в крокодиле...

— Но ведь это непредвиденный случай, — начал было я в весьма понятном волнении.

— Ах, нет, не говорите, не хочу, не хочу! — закричала она, вдруг совсем рассердившись. — [...] Мне уж чужие говорят, что мне развод дадут, потому что Иван Матвеич теперь уже не будет получать жалованья.

— Елена Ивановна! Вас ли я слышу? — закричал я патетически. — [...] Да и развод по такой неосновательной причине, как жалование, совершенно невозможен. А бедный, бедный Иван Матвеич к вам, так сказать, весь пылает любовью, даже и в недрах чудовища. [...] Ещё вчера ввечеру, [...] он упоминал, что в крайнем случае, может быть, решится выписать вас в качестве законной супруги к себе, в недра, тем более что крокодил оказывается весьма поместительным не только для двух, но даже и для трёх особ... [...]

— Как, как! — вскричала она в удивлении — Вы хотите, чтоб и я также полезла туда, к Ивану Матвеичу? Вот выдумки! Да и как я полезу, так в шляпке и в кринолине? Господи, какая глупость! Да и какую фигуру я буду делать, когда буду туда лезть, а на меня ещё кто-нибудь, пожалуй, будет смотреть... Это смешно! И что я там буду кушать?.. и... и как я там буду, когда..., ах боже мой, что они выдумали!.. [...]

think of next? ... [...] And what should I do if we quarrelled – should we have to go on lying there side by side? Foo, how horrid!"

"I agree, I agree with all those arguments, my sweet Elena Ivanovna," I interrupted [...]. "But one thing you have not appreciated in all this, you have not realized that he cannot live without you if he is inviting you there; that is proof of love, passionate, faithful, ardent love... [...]"

"I won't, I won't, I won't hear anything about it! [...] Get into it yourself, if you like the prospect. You're his friend, get in and keep him company, and spend your life discussing some boring science...."

"You are wrong to laugh at such a suggestion," I checked the frivolous woman with dignity. "lvan Matveich has invited me as it is." [...]

I described to her in detail all Ivan Matveich's plans. The thought of her evening receptions and her salon pleased her very much.

"Only I should need a great many new dresses," she observed," [...] Only ... only I don't know about that," she added thoughtfully. "How can he be brought here in the tank? That's very absurd. I don't want my husband to be carried about in a tank. I should feel quite ashamed for my visitors to see it... [...] By the way, you say Ivan Matveich spoke several times of me yesterday?"

"N-no, not exactly.... I must say he is thinking more now of the fate of humanity, and wants..."

"Oh, let him! You needn't go on! I'm sure it's terribly boring. I'll go and see him some time. I shall certainly go tomorrow. Only not today; I've got a headache, and besides, there will be such a lot of people there today.... They'll say, 'That's his wife,' and I shall feel ashamed..." [...]

At the office, of course, I gave no sign of being consumed by these cares and anxieties. But soon I noticed some of the most progressive papers seemed to be passing particularly rapidly from hand to hand among my colleagues, and were being read with an extremely serious expression of face.[...] The first one that reached me was the *News Sheet*, a paper of no particular party but humanitarian in general, for which it

И как же я буду, если мы там с ним поссоримся, — всё-таки рядом лежать? Фу, как это противно!

— Согласен, согласен со всеми этими доводами, милейшая Елена Ивановна, — прервал я — но вы не оценили одного во всём этом; вы не оценили того, что он, стало быть, без вас жить не может, коли зовёт туда; значит, тут любовь, любовь страстная, верная, стремящаяся... [...]

— Не хочу, не хочу, и слышать ничего не хочу! [...] Полезайте сами, если это вам приятно. Ведь вы друг, ну и ложитесь там с ним рядом из дружбы, и спорьте всю жизнь о каких-нибудь скучных науках...

— Напрасно вы так смеётесь над сим предположением, — с важностию остановил я легкомысленную женщину, — Иван Матвеич и без того меня звал туда. [...]

я подробно рассказал ей все вчерашние планы Ивана Матвеича. Мысль о приёмных вечерах и об открытом салоне ей очень понравилась.

— Но только надо будет очень много новых платьев, — заметила она, — [...] Только... только как же это, — прибавила она в раздумье, — как же это его будут приносить ко мне в ящике? это очень смешно. Я не хочу, чтоб моего мужа носили в ящике. Мне будет очень стыдно пред гостями... [...] Да, кстати, вы говорите, Иван Матвеич часто обо мне вчера говорил?

— Н-н-нет, не то чтобы очень... Признаюсь вам, он более думает теперь о судьбах всего человечества и хочет...

— Ну и пусть его! Подоговаривайте! Верно, скука ужасная. Я как-нибудь его навещу. Завтра непременно поеду. Только не сегодня; голова болит, а к тому же там будет так много публики... Скажут: это жена его, пристыдят... [...]

В канцелярии я, разумеется, не подал и виду, что меня пожирают такие заботы и хлопоты. Но вскоре заметил я, что некоторые из прогрессивнейших газет наших как-то особенно скоро переходили в это утро из рук в руки моих сослуживцев [...]. Первая попавшаяся мне была — «Листок», газетка без всякого особого направления, а так только

was regarded with contempt amongst us […]. Not without surprise I read in it the following paragraph:

"Yesterday strange rumors were circulating among the expansive and sumptuous buildings of our capital. A certain N., a well-known bon-vivant of the highest society, probably weary of the cuisine at Borel's and at the X. Club, went into the Passazh, into the place where an immense crocodile recently brought to the capital is being exhibited, and insisted on its being prepared for his dinner. After bargaining with the proprietor he at once set to work to devour him (that is, not the proprietor, a very meek and punctilious German, but his crocodile), cutting juicy morsels with his penknife from the living animal, and swallowing them with extraordinary rapidity. [...] We are by no means opposed to that new article of diet with which foreign gourmands have long been familiar. We even predicted it in advance. English lords and travellers make up regular parties for catching crocodiles in Egypt, and consume the monster's back cooked like beef-steak, with mustard, onions and potatoes. The French [...] prefer the paws baked in hot ashes [...]. For our part, we are delighted at a new branch of industry, of which our great and varied fatherland stands pre-eminently in need. Probably before a year is out crocodiles will be brought in hundreds to replace this first one, lost in the stomach of a Petersburg gourmand. And why should not the crocodile be acclimatized among us in Russia? If the waters of the Neva are too cold for these interesting strangers, there are ponds in the capital and rivers and lakes outside it. [...] While providing agreeable, wholesome nourishment for our fastidious gourmands, they might at the same time entertain the ladies who walk about these ponds and instruct the children in natural history. The crocodile skin might be used for making jewel-cases, boxes, cigar-cases, and pocket-books [...]. We hope to return more than once to this interesting topic."

Though I had foreseen something of the sort, the reckless inaccuracy of the paragraph overwhelmed me. [...] I turned to Prokhor Savvich who was sitting opposite to me, and noticed that […] in his hand he held the *Hairald*

вообще́ гума́нная, за что её преиму́щественно у нас презира́ли [...]. Не без удивле́ния прочёл я в ней сле́дующее:

«Вчера́ в на́шей обши́рной и украшённой великоле́пными зда́ниями столи́це распространи́лись чрезвыча́йные слу́хи. Не́кто N., изве́стный гастроно́м из вы́сшего о́бщества, вероя́тно наску́чив ку́хнею Боре́ля и — ского клу́ба, вошёл в зда́ние Пасса́жа, в то ме́сто, где пока́зывается огро́мный, то́лько что привезённый в столи́цу крокоди́л, и потре́бовал, чтоб ему́ изгото́вили его́ на обе́д. Сторгова́вшись с хозя́ином, он ту́т же приня́лся пожира́ть его́ (то́ есть не хозя́ина, весьма́ сми́рного и скло́нного к аккура́тности не́мца, а его́ крокоди́ла) — ещё живьём, отреза́я со́чные куски́ перочи́нным но́жичком и глота́я их с чрезвыча́йною поспе́шностью.[...] Мы во́все не про́тив сего́ но́вого проду́кта, давно́ уже́ изве́стного иностра́нным гастроно́мам. Мы да́же предска́зывали э́то наперёд. Англи́йские ло́рды и путеше́ственники ло́вят в Еги́пте крокоди́лов це́лыми па́ртиями и употребля́ют хребе́т чудо́вища в ви́де бифште́кса, с горчи́цей, лу́ком и карто́фелем. Францу́зы [...] предпочита́ют ла́пы, испечённые в горя́чей золе́ [...]. С свое́й стороны́, мы ра́ды но́вой о́трасли промы́шленности, кото́рой по преиму́ществу недостаёт на́шему си́льному и разнообра́зному оте́честву. Вслед за сим пе́рвым крокоди́лом, исче́знувшим в не́драх петербу́ргского гастроно́ма, вероя́тно, не пройдёт и го́да, как навезу́т их к нам со́тнями. И почему́ бы не акклиматизи́ровать крокоди́ла у нас в Росси́и? е́сли не́вская вода́ сли́шком холодна́ для сих интере́сных чужестра́нцев, то в столи́це име́ются пруды́, а за го́родом ре́чки и озёра. [...] Доставля́я прия́тную и здоро́вую пи́щу на́шим утончённым гастроно́мам, они́ в то же вре́мя могли́ бы увеселя́ть гуля́ющих на сих пруда́х дам и поуча́ть собо́ю дете́й есте́ственной исто́рии. Из крокоди́ловой ко́жи мо́жно бы бы́ло приготовля́ть футля́ры, чемода́ны, папиро́сочницы и бума́жники [...]. Наде́емся ещё не ра́з возврати́ться к э́тому интере́сному предме́ту».

Я хоть и предчу́вствовал что́-нибудь в э́том ро́де, тем не ме́нее опроме́тчивость изве́стия смути́ла меня́. [...] я обрати́лся к сиде́вшему напро́тив меня́ Про́хору Са́ввичу и заме́тил, что тот [...] в рука́х держа́л

as though he were on the point of passing it to me. [...] This was what I read in the *Hairald*:

"Everyone knows that we are progressive and humanitarian and want to be on a level with Europe in this respect. But in spite of all our exertions and the efforts of our paper we are still far from maturity, as may be judged from the shocking incident which took place yesterday in the Passazh and which we predicted long ago. A foreigner arrives in the capital bringing with him a crocodile which he begins exhibiting to the public in the Passazh. We immediately hasten to welcome a new branch of useful industry such as our powerful and varied fatherland stands in great need of. Suddenly yesterday at four o'clock in the afternoon a gentleman of exceptional stoutness enters the foreigner's shop in an intoxicated condition, pays his entrance fee, and immediately, without any warning, leaps into the jaws of the crocodile, who was forced, of course, to swallow him [...]. Tumbling into the inside of the crocodile, the stranger at once dropped asleep. [...] Within the crocodile was heard nothing but laughter and a promise to flay him (sic), though the poor mammal, compelled to swallow such a mass, was vainly shedding tears. An uninvited guest is worse than a Tartar. But, in spite of the proverb, the insolent visitor would not leave. We do not know how to explain such barbarous incidents, which prove our immaturity and disgrace us in the eyes of foreigners. The recklessness of the Russian temperament has found a fresh outlet. It may be asked what was the object of the uninvited visitor? [...] We would call our readers' attention to the barbarous treatment of domestic animals: it is difficult, of course, for the crocodile to digest such a mass all at once, and now he lies swollen out to the size of a mountain, awaiting death in insufferable agonies. In Europe persons guilty of inhumanity towards domestic animals have long been punished by law. But in spite of our European enlightenment, in spite of our European pavements, in spite of the European architecture of our houses, we are still far from shaking off our time-honoured prejudices." [...]

«Во́лос», как бы гото́вясь мне переда́ть его́. [...] Во́т что я прочёл в пока́занном ме́сте «Во́лоса»:

«Всем изве́стно, что мы прогресси́вны и гума́нны и хоти́м угоня́ться в э́том за Евро́пой. Но, несмотря́ на все на́ши стара́ния и на уси́лия на́шей газе́ты, мы ещё далеко́ не «созре́ли», как о то́м свиде́тельствует возмути́тельный факт, случи́вшийся вчера́ в Пасса́же и о кото́ром мы зара́нее предска́зывали. Приезжа́ет в столи́цу иностра́нец-со́бственник и привóзит с собо́й крокоди́ла, кото́рого и начина́ет пока́зывать в Пасса́же пу́блике. Мы тотча́с же поспеши́ли приве́тствовать но́вую о́трасль поле́зной промы́шленности, кото́рой вообще́ недостаёт на́шему си́льному и разнообра́зному оте́честву. Как вдру́г вчера́, в полови́не пя́того пополу́дни, в магази́н иностра́нца-со́бственника явля́ется не́кто необыча́йной толщины́ и в нетре́звом ви́де, пла́тит за вход и тотча́с же, безо́ вся́кого предуведомле́ния, ле́зет в пасть крокоди́ла, кото́рый, разуме́ется, принуждён был проглоти́ть его́ [...]. Ввали́вшись во вну́тренность крокоди́ла, незнако́мец тотча́с же засыпа́ет. [...] Из внутри́ крокоди́ла слы́шен лишь хо́хот и обеща́ние распра́виться ро́згами (sic), а бе́дное млекопита́ющее, принуждённое проглоти́ть таку́ю ма́ссу, тще́тно пролива́ет слёзы. Незва́ный гость ху́же тата́рина, но, несмотря́ на посло́вицу, наха́льный посети́тель выходи́ть не хо́чет. Не зна́ем, ка́к и объясни́ть подо́бные ва́рварские фа́кты, свиде́тельствующие о на́шей незре́лости и мара́ющие нас в глаза́х иностра́нцев. Разма́шистость ру́сской нату́ры нашла́ себе́ досто́йное примене́ние. Спра́шивается, чего́ хоте́лось непро́шенному посети́телю? [...] Обраща́ем ещё внима́ние на́ших чита́телей и на са́мое ва́рварство обраще́ния с дома́шними живо́тными: зае́зжему крокоди́лу, разуме́ется, тру́дно перевари́ть подо́бную ма́ссу ра́зом, и тепе́рь он лежи́т, разду́тый горо́й, и в нестерпи́мых страда́ниях ожида́ет сме́рти. В Евро́пе давно́ уже́ пресле́дуют судо́м обраща́ющихся негума́нно с дома́шними живо́тными. Но, несмотря́ на европе́йское освеще́ние, на европе́йские тротуа́ры, на европе́йскую постро́йку домо́в, нам ещё до́лго не отста́ть от заве́тных на́ших предрассу́дков.» [...]

"What's this? [...] Why, upon my word! Instead of pitying Ivan Matveich, they pity the crocodile!"

[...] And though the evening was far off, I slipped out of the office early to go to the Passazh and look, if only from a distance, at what was going on there, and to listen to the various remarks and currents of opinion. I foresaw there would be a regular crush there, and turned the collar of my coat right up to cover my face, as I somehow felt rather shy – so unused are we to publicity. But I feel I have no right to report my own prosaic feelings when faced with this remarkable and original incident.

Translation by Constance Garnett
Edited and updated by Sarah Young

— Что же это. […] Да поми́луйте, че́м бы об Ива́не Матве́иче пожале́ть, жале́ют о крокоди́ле.

[…] и хотя́ до ве́чера было ещё далеко́, но на э́тот раз я пора́ньше улизну́л из канцеля́рии, чтоб побыва́ть в Пасса́же и хоть и́здали посмотре́ть, что́ там де́лается, подслу́шать ра́зные мне́ния и направле́ния. Предчу́вствовал я, что там це́лая да́вка, и на вся́кий слу́чай поплотне́е заверну́л лицо́ в воротни́к шине́ли, потому́ что мне бы́ло чего́-то немно́го сты́дно — до того́ мы не привы́кли к публи́чности. Но чу́вствую, что я не впра́ве передава́ть со́бственные, прозаи́ческие мои́ ощуще́ния ввиду́ тако́го замеча́тельного и оригина́льного собы́тия.

Fyodor Dostoyevsky, 1863

Letter to Sofya
Fyodor Dostoyevsky

In February 1867 Dostoyevsky married Anna Snitkina, the secretary who had helped him complete work on the novella *The Gambler* to fulfil a contract taken out in desperate times with an unscrupulous publisher, to whom he would otherwise forfeit the rights to all his works. Debts forced the couple to leave Russia, and they spent the next four chaotic and traumatic years living in Europe. Dostoyevsky's gambling and frequent attacks of epilepsy interrupted his work and exacerbated their financial problems, and the birth and death of their first daughter turned hope into despair. During this period Dostoyevsky was working on *The Idiot*. He struggled at first to establish his subject matter, the hero of his early notes bearing little relation to the humility of Prince Myshkin in the final version. In this letter, sent to his favorite niece shortly before the first part of the serial publication appeared, he describes the thinking behind his central character. At this point, having completed part one of the novel, Dostoyevsky had little idea about how it would continue and, remarkably, he wrote the remaining parts without an overall plan.

To S.A. Ivanova

Geneva, January 1 (13), 1868

My entire fate rests on my work. Furthermore, I took an advance of approximately 4,500 rubles from *The Russian Messenger* and gave the editors my word of honor and repeated for an entire year in every letter to them that the novel would come. And just when I was on the verge of sending the novel off to the journal, I had to scrap it because I didn't like it anymore. (And if I don't like it anymore, I can't do a good job of writing it.) I've destroyed much of what I wrote. Meanwhile, the payment of my debt, my basic survival, and my entire future are tied up in the novel. Then, about three weeks ago (December 18 new style), I took up writing another novel and began working on it day and night. The idea for the novel is old and dear to me, but so difficult that I didn't dare start working on it, and absolutely the only reason I've started working on it now is that I'm in a state of near desperation. The main idea of the novel is to portray a positively beautiful man. There is nothing harder than this in the world, especially now. All writers, not only ours, but even European writers, whoever undertakes to portray the positively beautiful always gives up. Because this task is immense. The beautiful is an ideal, and both our ideal and that of civilized Europe are far from having been worked out. In the

С. А. ИВАНОВОЙ

Женева, 1 (13) января 1868 г.

… От работы моей зависит вся моя участь. Сверх того, я забрал около 4500 р. в Ред<акции> «Русского вестника» вперёд, а им честное слово дал и повторял его целый год во всяком письме в Редакцию, что роман будет. И вот, почти перед самой отсылкой в Редакцию романа, мне пришлось забраковать его, потому что он мне перестал нравиться. (А коли перестал нравиться, то нельзя написать хорошо). Я уничтожил много написанного. Между тем в романе и отдача моего долга, и жизнь насущная, и всё будущее заключалось. Тогда я, недели три тому назад (18-е декабря нового стиля), принялся за другой роман и стал работать день и ночь. Идея романа — моя старинная и любимая, но до того трудная, что я долго не смел браться за неё, а если взялся теперь, то решительно потому, что был в положении чуть не отчаянном. Главная мысль романа — изобразить положительно прекрасного человека. Труднее этого нет ничего на свете, а особенно теперь. Все писатели, не только наши, но даже все европейские, кто только ни брался за изображение положительно прекрасного, — всегда пасовал. Потому что это задача безмерная. Прекрасное есть идеал, а идеал — ни наш, ни цивилизованной Европы ещё далеко не выработался. На свете

world, the only positively beautiful person is Christ, so this phenomenon of the boundlessly, infinitely beautiful person is of course an infinite miracle in and of itself. (This idea underlies the entire Gospel of John; he finds the entire miracle in the incarnation alone, in the manifestation of the beautiful alone). But I'm getting carried away. I will just mention that of all the beautiful men in Christian literature, only *Don Quixote* is complete. But he is beautiful only because he was ridiculous at the same time. Dickens' *Pickwick* (an infinitely weaker idea compared with *Don Quixote*, but immense nevertheless) is also ridiculous, which is the only reason he works. Whenever there is compassion toward the ridiculed, toward un-self-conscious beauty, there will be sympathy in the reader. This arousal of compassion is the secret of humor. Jean Valjean is also a strong attempt, but he arouses sympathy because of his terrible misfortune and society's injustice toward him. I have nothing of the sort, absolutely nothing, and therefore I'm terribly afraid that this will be a positive failure. Some details may not be too bad. I fear that it will be tiresome. The novel is long. I wrote the entire first part in 23 days and sent it off just recently. It will be absolutely ineffective. Of course this is just the introduction, and it is good that nothing is compromised yet, but also almost nothing is explained, nothing is settled. My only desire is to arouse at least some curiosity in readers so that they take on the second part. I'll finish the second part, which I'm getting to work on today, in a month (I've been working that way all my life, after all). It seems to me that it will be stronger and a bit more solid than the first. Wish me, my dear friend, at least some sort of success! The name of the novel is *The Idiot*, and it is dedicated to you, that is, to Sofya Alexandrovna Ivanova. My dear friend, how I long for the novel to turn out to be at least somewhat worthy of its dedication. In any event, I cannot be my own judge, especially in the heat of the moment.

Translation by Nora Favorov

есть одно́ то́лько положи́тельно прекра́сное лицо́ Христо́с, та́к что явле́ние э́того безме́рно, бесконе́чно прекра́сного лица́ уж коне́чно есть бесконе́чное чу́до. (Все Ева́нгелие Иоа́нна в э́том смы́сле; он всё чу́до нахо́дит в одно́м воплоще́нии, в одно́м появле́нии прекра́сного). Но я сли́шком далеко́ зашёл. Упомяну́ то́лько, что из прекра́сных лиц в литерату́ре христиа́нской стои́т всего́ зако́нченное Дон Кихо́т. Но он прекра́сен еди́нственно потому́, что в то же вре́мя и смешо́н. Пи́квик Ди́ккенса (бесконе́чно слабе́йшая мы́сль, чем Дон Кихо́т; но всё-таки огро́мная) то́же смешо́н и тем то́лько и берёт. Явля́ется сострада́ние к осме́янному и не зна́ющему себе́ цены́ прекра́сному — а, ста́ло быть, явля́ется симпа́тия и в чита́теле. Э́то возбужде́ние сострада́ния и́ есть та́йна ю́мора. Жан Вальжа́н, то́же си́льная попы́тка, — но он возбужда́ет симпа́тию по ужа́сному своему́ несча́стью и несправедли́вости к нему́ о́бщества. У меня́ ничего́ нет подо́бного, ничего́ реши́тельно, и потому́ бою́сь стра́шно, что бу́дет положи́тельная неуда́ча. Не́которые дета́ли, мо́жет быть, бу́дут недурны́. Бою́сь, что бу́дет ску́чен. Рома́н дли́нный. Пе́рвую часть написа́л всю в 23 дня и на дня́х отосла́л. Она́ бу́дет реши́тельно не эффе́ктна. Коне́чно, э́то то́лько введе́ние, и хорошо́ то, что ничего́ ещё не скомпромети́ровано; но ничего́ почти́ и не разъяснено́, ничего́ не поста́влено. Моё еди́нственное жела́ние, — чтоб она́ хотя́ не́которое любопы́тство возбуди́ла в чита́теле, для того́, чтоб он взя́лся за втору́ю. Втору́ю, за кото́рую сажу́сь сего́дня, — око́нчу в ме́сяц (я и всю жи́знь ведь так рабо́тал). Мне ка́жется, она́ бу́дет покре́пче и покапита́льнее пе́рвой. Пожела́йте мне, ми́лый друг, хоть како́й-нибу́дь уда́чи! Рома́н называ́ется «Идио́т», посвящён Вам, то́ есть Со́фье Алекса́ндровне Ивано́вой. Ми́лый друг мой, как бы я жела́л, чтоб рома́н вы́шел хоть ско́лько-нибу́дь досто́ин посвяще́ния. Во вся́ком слу́чае, я себе́ сам не судья́, осо́бенно так сгоряча́, как тепе́рь. ...

Dostoyevsky Lived Here
Building on the corner of Grazhdanskaya ulitsa and Stolyarny pereulok,
as it looked at the end of the nineteenth century.

Fathers and Children

Son and father, vile Fyodor,
Both enamored of a whore,
Grushenka, a saintly sinner.
Mitya stakes his life to win her.
Katerina vows to wed him.
Think it's love? No, mental bedlam.
Enter others of the clan —
Mild Alyosha, grim Ivan.
Each night Fyodor awaits a visitor.
Time out for the Grand Inquisitor.
God's world sucks: it's hard to stick it!
Vanya's giving back his ticket.
Alyosha's faith is tried as well.
Zossima dies and starts to smell.
Fyodor is murdered! Money's gone!
Police suspect his oldest son.
Smerdyakov has done the killing.
Vanya's guilty—he was willing.
The trial proceeds with much ado.
Hearts alone can know what's true.
The law can't see the heart's interior:
Mitya's sentenced to Siberia.
Escape is planned but nothing's certain.
Cheer Alyosha; drop the curtain.

Lydia Razran Stone, 1970 (revised 2013)

Monument to Fyodor Dostoyevsky in Tallinn, Estonia.
Photo © Tony Bowden

Vlas

Fyodor Dostoyevsky

In the 1870s, between writing his novels *Demons, The Adolescent* and *The Brothers Karamazov,* Dostoyevsky spent several years working on *A Writer's Diary,* an experimental monthly journal for which he wrote all the material, combining short stories with art and literary criticism, commentary on current events, responses to readers' letters and other journalistic pieces. "Vlas" appeared in 1873, the first year of the publication. It begins as a curious, but apparently true, tale of a young peasant who is provoked into a committing a blasphemous act but is stopped by a vision of Christ's crucifixion, a conversion experience that leads him to beg for suffering for his sins. Beginning with the psychological and physiological aspects of the anecdote, Dostoyevsky turns the story into a discussion of the nature of Russian peasants, their capacity for sin as well as suffering, and the nature of Russian religious faith, reflecting the views he developed after spending four years living amongst the peasant convicts in the prison camp.

This is a true incident and its exceptionality alone makes it remarkable.

In the monasteries of Holy Russia there are, even now, people say, certain ascetics and monks who are confessors and who cast their light on us all....

Such an elder lives, let's suppose, in Kherson Province, and people come to him, some even on foot, from Petersburg, from Arkhangelsk, from the Caucasus, and from Siberia. They come, of course, with souls weighed down by despair, souls that no longer expect recovery; or they come bearing such a terrible burden in their hearts that the sinners can no longer speak about it to their own priest and spiritual father – not because of fear or mistrust, but simply out of utter despair for their own salvation. But then they hear about some such remarkable monk and they go to see him.

"And so it is," such an elder once said in friendly conversation with a certain listener, "that I have been listening to people for twenty years now, and you can believe how many things I have heard during these twenty years of my acquaintance with the most secret and complex ailments of the human soul. But even after twenty years I sometimes shudder and grow angry when I hear some secret confessions. You lose the spiritual calm that's needed to give comfort and have to restore your own humility and tranquility..."

[…] Происше́ствие э́то и́стинное и уже́ по одно́й свое́й необыкнове́нности замеча́тельное.

На Руси́, по монастыря́м, есть, говоря́т, и тепе́рь ины́е схи́мники, мона́хи — испове́дники и советода́тели. […]

Живёт э́тот ста́рец, поло́жим, в Хе́рсонской губе́рнии, а к нему́ е́дут и́ли да́же иду́т пешко́м из Петербу́рга, из Арха́нгельска, с Кавка́за и из Сиби́ри. Иду́т, разуме́ется, с разда́вленною отча́янием душо́ю, кото́рая уже́ и не ждёт себе́ исцеле́ния, и́ли с таки́м стра́шным бре́менем на се́рдце, что гре́шник уже́ и не говори́т о нем своему́ свяще́ннику-духо́внику, — не от стра́ха и́ли недове́рия, а про́сто в соверше́нном отча́янии за спасе́ние своё. А прослы́шит вдруг про како́го-нибу́дь тако́го мона́ха-советода́теля и пойдёт к нему́.

«И вот, — говори́л оди́н из таки́х ста́рцев одна́жды в дру́жеской бесе́де наедине́ с одни́м слу́шателем, — выслу́шиваю я люде́й два́дцать лет, и ве́рите ли, уж ско́лько, каза́лось бы, в два́дцать лет знако́мства моего́ с са́мыми потаёнными и сло́жными боле́знями души́ челове́ческой; но и че́рез два́дцать лет прихо́дишь иногда́ в содрога́ние и в негодова́ние, слу́шая ины́е та́йны. Теря́ешь необходи́мое споко́йствие ду́ха для пода́ния утеше́ния и сам вы́нужден себя́ же укрепля́ть в смире́нии и безмяте́жности...»

And then he told me this remarkable tale from the life of the People that I mentioned above.

It happened once that a peasant came crawling into my cell on his knees. I had already seen him through the window, crawling on the ground. The first thing he said to me was: "There's no salvation for me; I'm damned! Say what you like I'm damned all the same!"

I managed to calm him down. I could see that he had been crawling for the sake of the suffering and had crawled a great distance.

"A few of the lads got together in the village," he began, "and we set to arguing among ourselves as to which of us could do the most daring, shocking thing. I'm a proud fellow, and so I said I'd do worse than any of them. One of the lads took me aside and told me, face-to-face, 'You'd never ever do what you said; you're just bragging.'

"I told him I was ready to swear to it.

"'Just wait now,' he says, 'You have to swear by your own salvation in Heaven that you'll do everything I tell you.'

"I swore to it.

"'It'll soon be Lent,' he says, 'so make your fast. When you go to Holy Communion, take the Eucharist but don't swallow it. When you step back, take it out of your mouth and keep it. Then I'll tell you what else to do.'

"That's what I did. He took me straight from the church into a garden. He took a stick, drove it into the earfh, and said 'Put the Eucharist on the stick.' I did that.

"'Now,' he says, 'get a gun.'

"I brought one.

"'Load it.'

"I did that.

"'Take it up and shoot.'"

И ту́т-то он и рассказа́л ту удиви́тельную по́весть из наро́дного бы́та, о кото́рой я вы́ше упомяну́л.

«Ви́жу, вполза́ет ко мне раз мужи́к на коле́нях. Я ещё из окна́ ви́дел, как он полз по земле́. Пе́рвым сло́вом ко мне:

-Нет мне спасе́ния; про́клят! И что́ бы ты ни сказа́л — всё одно́ про́клят!

Я его́ кое-как успоко́ил; ви́жу, за страда́нием припо́лз челове́к; издалека́.

-Собрали́сь мы в дере́вне не́сколько парне́й, — на́чал он говори́ть, — и ста́ли проме́жду себя́ спо́рить: «Кто кого́ де́рзостнее сде́лает?» Я по го́рдости вы́звался пе́ред все́ми. Друго́й па́рень отвёл меня́ и говори́т мне с гла́зу на гла́з:

-э́то ника́к невозмо́жно тебе́, что́бы ты сде́лал, как говори́шь. Хва́стаешь.

Я ему́ стал кля́тву дава́ть.

— Нет, стой, покляни́сь, говори́т, свои́м спасе́нием на том све́те, что всё сде́лаешь, как я тебе́ укажу́.

Покля́лся.

— Тепе́рь ско́ро пост, говори́т, стань гове́ть. Когда́ пойдёшь к прича́стью — прича́стье прими́, но не проглоти́. Отойдёшь — вынь руко́й и сохрани́. А там я тебе́ укажу́.

Так я и сде́лал. Пря́мо из це́ркви повёл меня́ в огоро́д. Взял жёрдь, воткну́л в зе́млю и говори́т: положи́! Я положи́л на жёрдь.

— Тепе́рь, говори́т, принеси́ ружьё.

Я принёс.

— Заряди́.

Заряди́л.

— Подыми́ и вы́стрели.

"I raised the gun and aimed it. And, just as I was about to fire, I suddently saw before me a cross and, on it, the crucified Christ. Then I fell down, unconscious."

This had happened a few years before he came to the elder. Who was this Vlas?... Now isn't this a very typical incident that suggests a great deal, so that it's worthy of a few minutes of close examination? I still hold that these very same and sundry "Vlases," repentant and unrepentant, will say the last word; they will say it and will show us a new path and a new way out of all those apparently insoluble tangles we find ourselves in. Our Russian destiny will not be finally resolved by Petersburg. And therefore every *new* feature, even the smallest, that serves to characterize these "new people," may be worthy of our attention. [...]

The psychological aspect of the case is another matter. We have before us two national types that represent with full clarity the Russian People in their entirety. We see, first, the complete loss of a sense of measure in everything (and note that this is nearly always something temporary and passing that seems like the work of some evil power). There is an urge to go beyond the limit, an urge for that sinking sensation one has when one has come to the edge of an abyss, leans halfway over it, looks into the bottomless pit itself, and – in some particular but not infrequent cases – throws oneself headlong into it like a madman. We see this urge for negation in a person who may be the most inclined toward belief and reverence – the urge to negate everything: those things his heart holds most sacred, all those things the People cherish in totality, a thing which only a moment earlier had been an object of worship but which now suddenly seems an unbearable burden. What is especially striking is the haste and impetuosity with which the Russian reveals himself – in his good or his evil aspects – in certain characteristic moments of his own life or the life of the nation. Sometimes he simply can't be held back. Whether it is a matter of love or of drink, of debauchery, egoism, or envy – some Russians will surrender themselves utterly and totally, ready to break their links with

Я по́днял ру́ку и наме́тился. И вот то́лько бы вы́стрелить, вдруг предо́ мно́ю как есть крест, а на нём Распя́тый. Тут я и упа́л с ружьём в бесчу́вствии».

Происходи́ло э́то ещё за не́сколько лет до прихо́да к ста́рцу. Кто был э́тот Влас, отку́да и как его́ и́мя — ста́рец, разуме́ется, не откры́л [...]. Не пра́вда ли, что происше́ствие да́же весьма́ характе́рное с одно́й стороны́, на мно́гое намека́ющее, та́к что, пожа́луй, и сто́ит двух-трёх мину́т осо́бенного разбо́ра. Я всё того́ мне́ния, что ведь после́днее сло́во ска́жут они́ же, вот э́ти са́мые ра́зные «Вла́сы», ка́ющиеся и нека́ющиеся; они́ ска́жут и ука́жут нам но́вую доро́гу и но́вый исхо́д из всех, каза́лось бы, безысхо́дных затрудне́ний на́ших. Не Петербу́рг же разреши́т оконча́тельную судьбу́ ру́сскую. А потому́ вся́кая, да́же мале́йшая, но́вая черта́ об э́тих тепе́рь уже́ «но́вых лю́дях» мо́жет быть досто́йна внима́ния на́шего. [...]

Друго́е де́ло психологи́ческая часть фа́кта. Тут явля́ются пе́ред на́ми два наро́дные ти́па, в вы́сшей сте́пени изобража́ющие нам весь ру́сский наро́д в его́ це́лом. Э́то пре́жде всего́ забве́ние вся́кой ме́рки во всём (и, заме́тьте, всегда́ почти́ вре́менное и проходя́щее, явля́ющееся как бы каки́м-то наважде́нием). Э́то потре́бность хвати́ть че́рез край, потре́бность в замира́ющем ощуще́нии, дойдя́ до про́пасти, све́ситься в неё наполови́ну, загляну́ть в са́мую бе́здну и — в ча́стных слу́чаях, но весьма́ нере́дких — бро́ситься в неё как ошале́лому вниз голово́й. Э́то потре́бность отрица́ния в челове́ке, иногда́ са́мом неотрица́ющем и благогове́ющем, отрица́ния всего́, са́мой гла́вной святы́ни се́рдца своего́, са́мого по́лного идеа́ла своего́, всей наро́дной святы́ни во все́й её полноте́, пе́ред кото́рой сейча́с лишь благогове́л и кото́рая вдруг как бу́дто ста́ла ему́ невыноси́мым каки́м-то бре́менем. Осо́бенно поража́ет та торопли́вость, стреми́тельность, с кото́рою ру́сский челове́к спеши́т иногда́ заяви́ть себя́, в ины́е характе́рные мину́ты свое́й и́ли наро́дной жи́зни, заяви́ть себя́ в хоро́шем и́ли в пога́ном. Иногда́ тут про́сто нет уде́ржу. Любо́вь ли, вино́ ли, разгу́л, самолю́бие, за́висть — тут ино́й

everything and renounce everything: family, custom, God. The kindest man may suddenly be transformed into a vile reprobate and criminal; he needs only to be caught up by this whirlwind, this fateful maelstrom of violent and momentary negation and destruction of self that is so typical of the Russian national character at certain fateful moments in its existence. On the other hand, it is with the same force, the same impetuosity, the same urge for self-preservation and repentance that the Russian, like the Russian People as a whole, saves himself; he does this usually when he reaches the outermost limit, that is, when he has nowhere farther to go. Especially characteristic is the fact that this impulse backward, the impulse to restore and save oneself, is always more serious than the former urge to deny and destroy the self. Accordingly, the urge to destroy can be charged to a petty meanness of spirit; but the Russian sets about restoring himself with the most enormous and serious effort, and has only contempt for himself in his former movement toward negation.

I think that the principal and most basic spiritual need of the Russian People is the need for suffering, incessant and unslakeable suffering, everywhere and in everything. I think the Russian People have been infused with this need to suffer from time immemorial. A current of martyrdom runs through their entire history, and it flows not only from external misfortunes and disasters but springs from the very heart of the people themselves. There is always an element of suffering even in the happiness of the Russian People and without it their happiness is incomplete. Never, not even in the most triumphant moments of their history, do they assume a proud and triumphant air; they have an air of tenderness that almost reaches the point of suffering; the People sigh and attribute their glory to the mercy of the Lord. The Russian People seem to take delight in their sufferings. What is true of the entire People is also true of individuals, generally speaking at least. Consider, for example, the many types of Russian wrongdoers. Here one finds not only debauchery taken to an extreme, debauchery that is sometimes amazing in its bold sweep and in the abominable depths to which a human soul can sink. The wrongdoer is, first of all, a suffering

русский человек отдаётся почти беззаветно, готов порвать всё, отречься от всего, от семьи, обычая, бога. Иной добрейший человек как-то вдруг может сделаться омерзительным безобразником и преступником, — стоит только попасть ему в этот вихрь, роковой для нас круговорот судорожного и моментального самоотрицания и саморазрушения, так свойственный русскому народному характеру в иные роковые минуты его жизни. Но зато с такого же силою, с такого же стремительностью, с такою же жаждою самосохранения и покаяния русский человек, равно как и весь народ, и спасает себя сам, и обыкновенно, когда дойдёт до последней черты, то есть когда уже идти больше некуда. Но особенно характерно то, что обратный толчок, толчок восстановления и самоспасения, всегда бывает серьёзнее прежнего порыва — порыва отрицания и саморазрушения. То есть то бывает всегда на счету как бы мелкого малодушия; тогда как в восстановление своё русский человек уходит с самым огромным и серьёзным усилием, а на отрицательное прежнее движение своё смотрит с презрением к самому себе.

Я думаю, самая главная, самая коренная духовная потребность русского народа есть потребность страдания, всегдашнего и неутолимого, везде и во всём. Этою жаждою страдания он, кажется, заражён искони веков. Страдальческая струя проходит через всю его историю, не от внешних только несчастий и бедствий, а бьёт ключом из самого сердца народного. У русского народа даже в счастье непременно есть часть страдания, иначе счастье его для него неполно. Никогда, даже в самые торжественные минуты его истории, не имеет он гордого и торжествующего вида, а лишь умилённый до страдания вид; он воздыхает и относит славу свою к милости господа. Страданием своим русский народ как бы наслаждается. Что в целом народе, то и в отдельных типах, говоря, впрочем, лишь вообще. Вглядитесь, например, в многочисленные типы русского безобразника. Тут не один лишь разгул через край, иногда удивляющий дерзостью своих пределов и мерзостью падения души человеческой. Безобразник этот прежде всего сам страдалец. Наивно-торжественного довольства собою в русском

person himself. There is no naïvely gloating self-satisfaction in the Russian, even if he is a fool. Compare a Russian drunkard with the German one for example: the Russian is far more foul than the German, but the German is certainly the more stupid and ridiculous of the two. [...] The drunken German is definitely a happy man and he never weeps; he sings songs boasting of his prowess and is proud of himself. He comes home drunk as a cobbler, but still proud of himself. The Russian likes to drink from grief and to weep. And if he does put on airs, it's not because he's gloating; he only wants to raise a ruckus. He'll always recall some past insult and hurl reproaches at the one who insulted him, whether that person is present or not. He may brazenly insist that he's the next thing to a general; he'll swear like a trooper if you don't believe him, and finally he'll shout for someone to come and help him convince you. Yet the reason he presents such an ugly spectacle, the reason he wants someone to help him, is that in the depths of his drunken soul he knows very well that he's not a general but only a vile drunkard who has sunk to a level lower than any animal. What's true of one tiny instance is also true of much more important ones. The worst wrongdoer, even the one whose brazen and refined vices seem so attractive that other fools follow his example, still has some secret sense, in the depths of his deformed soul, that in the final analysis he's nothing more than a wretch. He's not complacent; reproach wells up in his heart, and he takes his revenge for it on those around him; he rages and attacks everyone. So it is that he pushes himself to the limit: as he grapples with the suffering that is constantly building up in his heart; at the same time he seems to revel with delight in his suffering. If he has the capacity to rise up out of his fallen state, then he exacts a terrible vengeance on himself for his past fall, an even more painful vengeance than he had exacted on others for the secret torments his own dissatisfaction with himself caused him while befogged in his degradation.

Who provided the impulse to set both these peasant lads to disputing which could commit the most brazen sin? What were the reasons that led to such a contest? These things remain a mystery, but there can be

челове́ке совсе́м да́же нет, да́же в глу́пом. Возьми́те ру́сского пья́ницу и, наприме́р, хоть неме́цкого пья́ницу: ру́сский па́костнее неме́цкого, но пья́ный не́мец несомне́нно глупе́е и смешне́е ру́сского. […] Пья́ный не́мец несомне́нно счастли́вый челове́к и никогда́ не пла́чет; он поёт самохва́льные пе́сни и горди́тся собо́ю. Прихо́дит домо́й пья́ный как сте́лька, но го́рдый собо́ю. Ру́сский пья́ница лю́бит пить с го́ря и пла́кать. Е́сли же кура́жится, то не торжеству́ет, а лишь буя́нит. Всегда́ вспо́мнит каку́ю-нибу́дь оби́ду и упрека́ет оби́дчика, тут ли он, нет ли. Он де́рзостно, пожа́луй, дока́зывает, что он чуть ли не генера́л, го́рько руга́ется, е́сли ему́ не ве́рят, и, что́бы уве́рить, в конце́ концо́в всегда́ зовёт «карау́л». Но ведь потому́ он так и безобра́зен, потому́ и зовёт «карау́л», что в тайника́х пья́ной души́ свое́й наве́рно сам убеждён, что он во́все не «генера́л», а то́лько га́дкий пья́ница и опа́костился ни́же вся́кой скоти́ны. Что в микроскопи́ческом приме́ре, то и в кру́пном. Са́мый кру́пный безобра́зник, са́мый да́же краси́вый свое́ю де́рзостью и изя́щными поро́ками, так что ему́ да́же подража́ют глупцы́, всё-таки слы́шит каки́м-то чутьём, в тайника́х безобра́зной души́ свое́й, что в конце́ концо́в он лишь негодя́й и то́лько. Он недово́лен собо́ю; в се́рдце его́ нараста́ет попрёк, и он мсти́т за него́ окружа́ющим; бесну́ется и ме́чется на всех, и тут-то вот и дохо́дит до кра́ю, боря́сь с накопля́ющимся ежемину́тно в се́рдце страда́нием свои́м, а вме́сте с тем и как бы упива́ясь им с наслажде́нием. Е́сли он спосо́бен восста́ть из своего́ униже́ния, то мсти́т себе́ за про́шлое паде́ние ужа́сно, да́же больне́е, чем вымеща́л на други́х в чаду́ безобра́зия свои́ та́йные му́ки от со́бственного недово́льства собо́ю.

Кто натолкну́л обо́их парне́й на спор о том: «Кто сде́лает де́рзостнее?» — и каки́ми причи́нами сложи́лась возмо́жность подо́бного состяза́ния

no doubt that both lads suffered – by accepting the challenge, the other by offering it. [...]

They could have found some other deed – something very shocking – for their contest: a robbery, a murder, open rebellion against some powerful person. The lad swore, after all, that he was ready for anything, and his tempter knew that a serious promise had been made, one that would be kept.

But no. The tempter thinks the most dreadful acts are too ordinary. He invents some unthinkable sin, unprecedented and inconceivable, and his choice reveals the People's whole outlook on life.

Inconceivable? Yet the very fact that he had decided on this, specifically, shows that he had perhaps been considering it already. This fanciful notion had crept into his soul long ago, perhaps even in his childhood; he was struck by the horror of it, yet also found it agonizingly delightful. [...]

There are many things one cannot conceive but only feel. There is a great deal one can know unconsciously. [...] It would also be good to know how he regarded himself: did he feel more to blame than his victim? As far as we can judge by his mentality, we must suppose that he regarded himself as more to blame, or at least equally to blame, so that when challenging his victim to this "brazen act," he was challenging himself as well.

We hear that the Russian People know the Gospels poorly and that they do not know the fundamental principles of our faith. That's true, of course, but they do know Christ and they have borne Him in their hearts from time immemorial. [...]Perhaps the only love of the Russian People is Christ, and they love His image in their own fashion, that is, to the point of suffering. [...]

And so to make a mockery of something the People hold so sacred, and thus to break one's links with the whole land; to destroy oneself forever through negation and pride solely for the sake of one moment of triumph – why the Russian Mephistopheles could invent nothing more daring! The prospect of such an extreme of passion, the prospect of such dark and complex sensations within the soul of a common, simple man is astounding! And remember that all this developed almost to the point of a conscious idea.

— осталось неизвестным, но несомненно, что оба страдали — один принимая вызов, другой предлагая его. […]

Можно было выбрать для состязания что-нибудь очень дерзкое и другого рода — разбой, убийство, открытое буйство против могущественного человека. Ведь поклялся же парень, что на всё пойдёт, и искуситель его знал, что на этот раз серьёзно говорено, впрямь пойдёт.

Нет. Самые страшные «дерзости» кажутся искусителю слишком обыкновенными. Он придумывает неслыханную дерзость, небывалую и немыслимую, и в её выборе выразилось целое мировоззрение народное.

Немыслимую? А между тем одно уже то, что он именно остановился на ней, показывает, что он уже, может быть, и мыслил о ней. Может быть, давно уже, с детства, эта мечта заползала в душу его, потрясала её ужасом, а вместе с тем и мучительным наслаждением. […]

Можно многое не сознавать, а лишь чувствовать. Можно очень много знать бессознательно. […] Хорошо бы тоже узнать, как он считал себя: виновнее или нет своей жертвы? Судя по кажущемуся его развитию, надо полагать, что считал виновнее или по крайней мере равным по вине; так что, вызывая жертву на «дерзость», вызывал и себя.

Говорят, русский народ плохо знает Евангелие, не знает основных правил веры. Конечно так, но Христа он знает и носит его в своём сердце искони. […] Может быть, единственная любовь народа русского есть Христос, и он любит образ его по-своему, то есть до страдания. […]

И вот надругаться над такой святыней народною, разорвать тем со всею землёй, разрушить себя самого во веки веков для одной лишь минуты торжества отрицаньем и гордостью — ничего не мог выдумать русский Мефистофель дерзостнее! Возможность такого напряжения страсти, возможность таких мрачных и сложных ощущений в душе простолюдина поражает! И заметьте, всё это возросло почти до сознательной идеи.

The victim, however, does not give in, is not humbled, is not frightened. At least he pretends that he isn't frightened. The lad accepts the challenge. [...] And now it is no longer a fanciful notion but a reality: he attends church; he hears the words of Christ every day, yet he does not shrink back. There are terrible murderers who are not daunted even by the sight of their victim. One such murderer, caught at the scene of the crime and guilty beyond any doubt, would not confess but kept lying to the investigating magistrate. And when the magistrate rose and ordered the man taken to prison, the murderer, with an air of utter tenderness, asked as a favor to be allowed to bid farewell to the woman he had murdered and whose body was still lying there (she was his former mistress, and he had killed her out of jealousy). He bent down, kissed her tenderly, and began to weep; still on his knees, he stretched his hands over her body and said once more that he was not guilty. I simply want to note that a man's feelings can atrophy to a brutish level.

But in the case in point there is no question of atrophy of feelings. Moreover, there is also something quite peculiar – mystical horror, the most colossal power over the human soul. [...] A sense of horror is something pitiless; it withers the heart and hardens it toward any lofty or tender feeling. And that is why the criminal was able to endure the moment before the communion chalice even though he may have been utterly paralyzed by fear. I also think that the mutual hatred of victim and tormentor totally vanished during these days. The tormented victim may have had pathological fits of hatred toward himself, those around him, and those who were praying in church, but least of all he hated his Mephistopheles. They both felt that they had need of one another so that together they might put an end to the affair. Each probably felt himself powerless to end it alone. Why, then, did they carry on? Why did they assume such a burden of torment? Yet they simply were unable to break their alliance. Had their contract been broken, they would at once have become inflamed with a mutual hatred ten times stronger than before, and there probably would have been a murder: the victim would have killed his tormentor.

Жёртва, одна́ко же, не сдаётся, не смиря́ется, не пуга́ется. По кра́йней ме́ре, де́лает вид, что не пуга́ется. Па́рень принима́ет вы́зов. […] Наступа́ет уже́ не мечта́, а са́мое де́ло: он хо́дит в це́рковь, слы́шит ежедне́вно слова́ Христо́вы и не отступа́ет. Быва́ют стра́шные уби́йцы, не смуща́ющиеся да́же при ви́де уби́той и́ми же́ртвы. Оди́н из таки́х уби́йц, я́вный и уличённый на ме́сте, не сознава́лся до конца́ и продолжа́л лга́ть пе́ред сле́дователем. Когда́ же тот встал и веле́л его́ отвести́ в остро́г, то он с умилённым ви́дом попроси́л как ми́лости прости́ться с лежа́вшею ту́т же уби́тою (его́ бы́вшею любо́вницею, кото́рую он уби́л из ре́вности). Он нагну́лся, поцелова́л её с умиле́нием, запла́кал и, не встава́я с коле́н, ещё раз повтори́л над не́ю, простира́я ру́ку, что он не вино́вен. Я то́лько хочу́ заме́тить, до како́й зве́рской сте́пени мо́жет доходи́ть в челове́ке бесчу́вственность.

Но здесь была́ совсе́м не бесчу́вственность. Све́рх того́, бы́ло ещё не́что совсе́м осо́бенное — мисти́ческий у́жас, са́мая огро́мная си́ла над душо́й челове́ческой. […] Ощуще́ние у́жаса есть чу́вство жёсткое, су́шит и камени́т се́рдце для вся́кого умиле́ния и высо́кого чу́вства. Вот почему́ престу́пник вы́держал и моме́нт пе́ред ча́щей, хотя́, мо́жет быть, и цепене́я от стра́ху до изнеможе́ния. И ду́маю то́же, что взаи́мная не́нависть ме́жду же́ртвой и её мучи́телем упа́ла в э́ти дни соверше́нно. Поры́вами искуша́емый мог с боле́зненною зло́стью ненави́деть себя́, окружа́ющих, моля́щихся в це́ркви, но всего́ ме́нее своего́ Мефисто́феля. о́ба они́ чу́вствовали, что взаи́мно друг в дру́ге нужда́ются, что́бы сообща́ ко́нчить де́ло. Ка́ждый, наве́рно, счита́л себя́ бесси́льным его́ ко́нчить оди́н. Для чего́ же они́ продолжа́ли его́, для чего́ же при́няли сто́лько му́ки? Они́ и не могли́, впро́чем, разорва́ть сою́з. Е́сли бы их контра́кт был нару́шен, то тотча́с же возгоре́лась бы взаи́мная не́нависть в де́сять раз сильне́е пре́жнего и, наве́рно, произошло́ бы уби́йство: му́ченик уби́л бы своего́ мучи́теля.

This could well have happened. Even murder would be nothing compared to the horror endured by the victim. The point is that deep within the souls of each of them there must have been some sort of infernal delight in their own perdition, the breath-catching urge to lean over the abyss and peer into it, a stupendous rapture at one's own temerity.[...]

Note also that the tempter did not reveal the whole secret to his victim: when he left the church he did not know what he was to do with the Eucharist until the very moment his tempter ordered him to get the gun. So many days of such mystical uncertainty again testify to this sinner's terrible obstinacy. On the other hand, our village Mephistopheles reveals himself a fine psychologist.

But perhaps when they came into the garden neither was aware of what he was doing? Still, the victim remembered loading and aiming the gun. Could he have only been acting mechanically, even though fully aware, as sometimes really happens when one is truly terrified? I do not think so: had he been transformed into a virtual machine that continues its operation only through force of inertia he would certainly not have had the vision that followed. He would simply have fallen down senseless once the full force of inertia had been exhausted – not before, but after the shooting. No, it's most likely that he was in a state of complete and extraordinarily lucid consciousness the whole time, despite the mortal dread that kept growing with every second. And the very fact that the victim endured such pressure of progressively growing horror is, I repeat, proof of his immense spiritual strength. [...]

The thunderous voice of judgment came out of his own heart of course. Why was it not expressed consciously? Why was there not a sudden parting of the clouds that had obscured his mind and his conscience? Why did it appear in an image that seemed entirely external, as a fact independent of his own spirit? We find here an immense psychological problem and an act of God. The criminal certainly saw this as an act of God. Our Vlas became a beggar and demanded suffering.

Пусть и это. Даже и это бы ничего перед вынесенным жертвою ужасом. То-то и есть, что тут должно было быть непременно на дне души и у того и у другого некоторое адское наслаждение собственной гибелью, захватывающая дыхание потребность нагнуться над пропастью и заглянуть в неё, потрясающее восхищение перед собственной дерзостью. […]

Заметьте ещё, что искуситель не открыл своей жертве всей тайны: она ещё не знала, выходя из церкви, что должна будет сделать с святыней, до самого того момента, как он велел принести ружье. Столько дней такой мистической неизвестности опять свидетельствуют об ужасном упорстве грешника. С другой стороны, и деревенский Мефистофель выказывает себя большим психологом.

Но, может быть, придя в огород, оба они уже не помнили себя? Парень помнил, однако, как заряжал ружье и наводил. Может быть, действовал лишь машинально, хотя и в полной памяти, как действительно бывает иногда в состоянии ужаса? Не думаю: если бы он обратился в одну лишь машину, продолжающую действовать по одной лишь инерции, то, наверно, не имел бы потом видения; просто упал бы без чувств, когда бы истощил весь запас инерции, — и не до, а уж после выстрела. Нет, вероятнее всего, что сознание сохранялось всё время в чрезвычайной ясности, несмотря на смертельный ужас, всё нараставший с каждым мгновением прогрессивно. И уже потому, что жертва выдержала такое давление ужаса, нараставшего прогрессивно, повторю опять, она была несомненно одарена огромною душевною силой. […]

Суд прогремел из его сердца конечно. Почему прогремел не сознательно, не внезапным прояснением ума и совести, почему проявился в образе, как бы совершенно внешним, независимым от его духа фактом? В этом огромная психологическая задача и дело господа. Для него, для преступника, без сомнения было делом господним. Влас пошёл по миру и потребовал страдания.

And what of the other Vlas, the tempter who was left? The story does not say that he came crawling after repentance; it says nothing about him. Perhaps he, too, came crawling; but perhaps he stayed on in his village and lives there now, still drinking and scoffing on church holidays: he did not see the vision, after all. But is that what really happened? I would very much like to know his story, just for the sake of information, as a subject for a sketch.

This is why I would like to know: what if he really and truly is a village nihilist, a homegrown cynic and thinker, an unbeliever who decided on such a contest with haughty mockery on his face, who did not suffer and tremble with his victim, as I suggest in this sketch, but who followed his victim's trembling and writhing with cold curiosity, solely out of a need to see someone else suffer, to see another man humiliated – who knows, perhaps even for the sake of scientific inquiry?

Translation by Kenneth Lantz

Ну а друго́й-то Влас, оста́вшийся, искуси́тель? Леге́нда не говори́т, что он попо́лз за покая́нием, не упомина́ет о нем ничего́. Мо́жет, попо́лз и он, а мо́жет, и оста́лся в дере́вне и живёт себе́ до сих по́р, опя́ть пьёт и зубоска́лит по пра́здникам: ведь не о́н же ви́дел виде́ние. Та́к ли, впро́чем? о́чень бы жела́тельно узна́ть и его́ исто́рию, для све́дения, для этю́да.

Во́т почему́ ещё жела́тельно бы: что, е́сли э́то и впря́мь настоя́щий нигили́ст дереве́нский, доморо́щенный отрица́тель и мысли́тель, не ве́рующий, с высокоме́рною насме́шкой вы́бравший предме́т состяза́ния, не страда́вший, не трепета́вший вме́сте с свое́ю же́ртвою, как предположи́ли мы в на́шем этю́де, а с холо́дным любопы́тством следи́вший за её трепета́ниями и ко́рчами, из одно́й ли́шь потре́бности чужо́го страда́ния, челове́ческого униже́ния, — черт зна́ет, мо́жет быть, из учёного наблюде́ния?

www.ingramcontent.com/pod-product-compliance
Lightning Source LLC
Chambersburg PA
CBHW061456210726
48287CB00007B/2536